THE PARAGON OF ANIMALS

SCOTT BACHMANN

Scott Comics
4300 Parklawn Drive
Kettering, OH, 45440
www.scottcomics.com
scott@scottcomics.com

First printing March 2012

ISBN 978-0-9896051-3-7

DEDICATION

To my wife Anita for always being there, and without whom I wouldn't be here, or anywhere.

To Glenn Jones who taught me Science Fiction and that both the Welsh and the Germans love their double consonants.

To Larry Niven, Jerry Pournelle, Ben Bova, Roger Zelazny, Piers Anthony, Philip José Farmer, Mark Twain, Robert Louis Stevenson, and Kurt Vonnegut for teaching me to love the written word.

To Warren Ellis, Brian Bendis, Jay O'Barr, Mark Waid, Neil Gaiman, Chris Claremont, Bill Mantlo, John Ney Rieber, Terry Moore and Doug Moench for teaching me to love the illustrated word.

To Seth, Aaron, Ruth, Lou, Lynne, and Dave for teaching me that I was not alone in my love for the illustrated word.

To Diana for encouragement and contacts.

To Dillo who always knew I could do this.

CONTENTS

1 1

2 15

3 24

4 41

5 50

6 61

7 76

8 89

9 107

10 118

11 134

12 152

13 174

EPILOGUE..186

ABOUT THE AUTHOR 190

ABOUT THE COVER 191

ACKNOWLEDGMENTS

The first edition of this work was edited by Skylar Burris. The second edition of this work was edited by William Boughton, Josh Pressnell, Heather Anderson, Crystal Kushmaul, Paul Lell, and Janine Rigg.

Scott D.M. Simmons and Diana Pressnell helped with the comic book version of Paragon, which influenced the novel.

"What a piece of work is a man, how noble in reason, how infinite in faculties, in form and moving how express and admirable, in action how like an angel, in apprehension how like a god -- the beauty of the world, the paragon of animals…"
~ William Shakespeare

"It is a given that Man is the noblest of all God's creatures. But you have to ask, who discovered that?"
~ Mark Twain

1

When Liza turned six in 1981, she was suddenly buried under a mountain of ridicule and nagging from her newly single mother and this miserable situation lasted until Liza finally left home at eighteen. It was always something. Liza's clothes were wrong. "You dress like a boy. Go back up there and put on a dress and then shave your damn legs for once." Her attitude was wrong. "Get your head out of that book and get your butt outside." Her look was wrong. "The only boy who'd bother to make out with you would have to be drunk, desperate, and fat." Her Mom thought she was doing what was best for Liza, trying to forge Liza into being the right kind of person, the kind no man would leave.

Not only was her mother a part of the daily ridicule, her older bother, by two years, would take his turn picking on Liza. Instead of getting in trouble for being a brat of a child, Mom thought Davey was a wonderful boy who could do no wrong. Mom was oblivious to the truth, no matter the evidence to the contrary. Davey was just behaving the way Mom thought all men behaved.

As fate would have it, David grew up tall and strong and made varsity as a wide receiver. Wherever he went he was surrounded by a gang of friends that continued to enable his misbehavior. They also mimicked him and picked on Liza whenever they were bored, which was always.

Worst of all was the ridicule she received from every female under the age of eighteen in their tiny town of Clarksdale, Ohio. In a small town, everyone knows everyone, and Liza was designated the runt of the town's litter, and she was never allowed to forget it. Fortunately, most of the females over eighteen were too busy to harass Liza. They were either married with children, trying to get married by bar cruising, or working double shifts at the engine factory at one of the few jobs they had left. Everyone else had been smart enough to move away at the first opportunity. Every female with one glaring exception: her best friend, Gwenifer Two Tales.

If Liza was the town's runt of the litter, Gwenifer was the cute goofy puppy who tripped over her own ears and whom everyone adored. Her birth certificate said her name was Jenny Jones, but no one called her that. From the day she learned to talk Two Tales always had two things to say about everything, and at some point the nickname stuck.

Gwenifer's first name wasn't a nickname; it was the name she chose for herself. Throughout elementary school, Jenny Jones hated her pedantic alliterative name. She'd fill out her school papers with variations like Jennifer, Jen, JJ, and Gwendolyn. By middle school she had settled on calling herself Gwenifer. The name change served two very important purposes to her: one, no one could spell it or pronounce it correctly which she found endlessly amusing, and two, the name regularly afforded her with something to talk about. Anything that gave Two Tales an excuse to talk was a thing she would treasure.

While Gwen was different, she was deemed to be of average intelligence based on her grades and standardized test scores. Liza, on the other hand, was prodded and measured by school psychologists and well meaning teachers who determined again and again that she was more than just smart: she was brilliant. She could have easily been valedictorian if she had "only applied herself" as every guidance counselor urged her to do. Instead, she was a solidly B+ girl. Liza got As in the subjects she liked, and F's in the subjects she did not.

What Liza did excel at was reading. She spent more time in the library than all of her classmates combined. She read classics at first, following Kipling to Twain and grudgingly Faulkner. She moved onto the modern masters, reading scandalous Updike and his Rabbit stories in the sixth grade, just before the First Baptists and the Reformation Lutherans had them removed them from the library once and for all. Once she'd deemed herself to be erudite enough, she dared to take on the more common genre sections of the library stacks.

Liza thumbed through the well picked-over hardboiled pulp mysteries of Hammet and Chandler, but she was eventually drawn to the glossy new hardbound books of gory forensic procedurals, such as Cornwell and Cook. Books so detailed in their ichor that she once passed a middle school biology exam without ever opening the chapter on anatomy. Ultimately she ended her meandering journey with lush escapist fantasies of high magic and dark evils. She'd worked her way from children's books such as *Narnia* and *Redwall* to marching through Middle Earth, taking a psychedelic detour through Amber and the World of Tiers, to prepare for the marathon of endless books by Marian Zimmer Bradley and Piers Anthony. In every case, no matter what the style, Liza found herself within the stories. She was the wise, but put-upon, outsider who had to prove herself against disbelief, who succeeded when all doubted. In her mind, Liza was the champion waiting for her cause, and Gwen was the adorable sidekick who never knew when to shut up.

Gwenifer, unlike Liza, was regarded by most as attractive. The best compliment Liza could elicit was that she was cute for a chubby girl. In contrast, a stiff wind could blow Gwenifer over without much difficulty. That said, Liza was only slightly overweight, and was fortunate enough to carry that weight in her curves, but she was also unfortunate enough that it showed in her cheeks and neck, creating an illusion that she was heavier than she was. Liza made things worse by wearing loose clothing in an attempt to hide herself, which made her silhouette look chunky instead of curvy. Many women in Clarksdale were significantly heavier than Liza, but Liza was the one everyone called fat.

Gwen liked to say their differences in size suited them because Gwenifer preferred her thoughts to be "airy" while Liza enjoyed "heavy pondering." Liza preferred to be a big thinker - tackling subjects in school debates and essays that other students didn't even know existed. Meanwhile, Gwenifer painted ethereal images in watercolors, lithe spirits with gossamer wings.

Gwen thought Liza was brilliant and would listen to her for hours, or so Gwen believed. If anyone kept track, Gwen was always the one doing the talking, usually about nothing much at all, but Liza never minded because she enjoyed having the company of someone who didn't look down on her. They were both social outcasts for different reasons, and they were both quite comfortable together.

If Liza had been given a choice in friends, however, she would not have picked Two Tales from a crowd of candidates. Gwen was kooky enough to get on even Liza's nerves, and there were times Liza deliberately put on headphones to drown her out. Gwen never noticed.

Occasionally a boy would chase after Two Tales, hoping he could dive into her pants and get back out "before the crazy stuck to him." During some of these times the boy would bring a friend along who'd be forced into the role of wingman and given the job of keeping Liza busy. This was the extent of Liza's dating experience: left-over wingmen who loved to play video games with her. The games never went well because they hated losing to a girl. Outside of video games they would stare at her breasts like a dog begging at the dinner table, but otherwise they had no use for her at all.

Liza wasn't stupid about men; she knew what the real problem was. She knew she was not ugly, or freakish, or lezzie, or any of the other words that mean girls scrawled on her books and locker. From what Liza could tell, ugly girls and crazy girls alike found dates eventually. Liza knew her problem was that she was smart, strong willed, and opinionated. Boys hated that. They were threatened by her, and so they called her a bitch and occasionally, for reasons Liza never understood, a whore. Liza took it all in stride. While other girls were out dating, she was at the library, or at home in her room. She pretended to be okay with that, and most of the time she was. Then came one of the worst days of her life: that day in the summer of 1990 when she let her hormones take over.

The boy who took her virginity was named Steve. It happened when Steve brought the beer to a party thrown by her brother, Dave (a party he wasn't supposed to have). They were all seventeen, except for Liza who was fifteen and a half. Liza's mom was away on a weekend-long date in Tennessee, camping in the hills with Steve's father. Her mom had met him at a church singles' picnic, and the two had shared "my divorce was better than yours" stories until they were dancing in a country bar, which then led to a well-gossiped-about make-out session in the cab of his pick-up in the bar's parking lot. Liza's mom insisted that the unseemly behavior would be made more seemly by out-of-town camping. Steve turned out to be a lot like his father, making sure everyone was drunk before eleven so his hand could be up every blouse by twelve. He seemed to like Liza's blouse the best, returning several times. She had enough beer in her at that point that she knew she could pee for twenty minutes straight if she tried, but she kept putting that off because Steve kept pawing at her and calling her "all woman and all good." He then made it clear, out loud, several times, that he needed to have his way with someone soon or he'd be forced to 'do it' with the cigarette hole that was burnt into the couch.

She snuck him up to her room, and soon wished that she hadn't. The sex was terrible and painful; all dry pounding and burping. It ended quickly without any climax on her part, while he insisted on spending himself all over her chest. When Steve became more interested in vomiting than in her nipples, she pushed him off of her. He staggered a bit then got sick in her wastebasket. Liza ran to the bathroom and locked the door and stayed there all night, ignoring any pounding on it from the other side.

That night Gwen slept with Liza's brother. They both had such a good time of it that Liza had to spend the next few years telling Gwen to shut up because whenever she thought about him or heard his name, Gwen would rhapsodize in explicit detail.

When Liza turned eighteen, she did her best to escape her life. She graduated early and went straight to community college on the state's dime because her mom couldn't afford anything else, and if mom could do anything at all, it would be to ensure that David could play for Ohio State.

Liza commuted back and forth to class by bus. It was an hour and a half each way with two connections, and a twenty-minute crossover between bus routes, a joy in Ohio winters. At night she slept on the couch in Gwen's apartment. The well-worn thing had been rescued from a curb before trash day because it was lavender and Gwen wouldn't let a lavender couch die.

Gwen didn't go to school because she had inherited almost enough to live on. Her family had passed away in a "car/train/I-can-beat-the-signal/alcohol" accident when Gwen was fifteen. She had lived for a while with an aunt, but, when she turned eighteen, the insurance policy kicked in and she started living on her own. As long as she didn't eat out or use electricity, she was fine. Gwen lived alone with her muse, which varied monthly in its forms. Sometimes she painted with a variety of media that was and was not paint. Sometimes she sculpted pottery no one would ever use or could even identify. Other times she made nude pictures of herself to draw attention to her more serious art, and to sell for a few dollars to pay for art supplies. She liked to play bass guitar and planned to play in a band one day if she could find someone who could both play lead guitar and endure her insistence on singing. Gwen was so tone-deaf only cats in heat could appreciate her stylings. Mostly, Gwen watched lots of cable TV, ate unhealthy food when she could afford it, and stubbornly defied physics and math by never gaining weight when she did.

Liza paid for part of the apartment with her student loans and grants. She also kept the place clean in spite of Gwen's free-spirited choice to never use a trash can. The apartment had once been a large farm house, but it had been carved into four suites, and this suite only had one bedroom, which meant that Liza had no real living space of her own. Liza did have her own desk in the corner with a creaky old PC, and she managed to scrape up enough to pay for luxuries like dial-up Internet, cable, and her cellphone minutes. It wasn't an ideal way to live, but for Liza, it was perfect.

Gwen was tallish for a girl, while Liza was on the short end of things. Gwen was a wispy pure blonde, but she was given to dying her hair a new color when the whim suited her and when she remembered to buy hair dye. Liza was a dishwater blonde with hair that varied from icky auburn to dirty yellow in the sun with a slight frizzy curl that never allowed her to do anything sane with it. She took to rolling it up under a baseball cap. Frustration would drive her to cut it off every once in awhile, which meant Liza had to endure the obligatory 'dyke' name-calling. Liza never had a problem with homosexuals, and she told herself to ignore it, but the bigoted taunts had an effect on her, made her feel ashamed. Gwen, on the other hand, was free spirited enough to try anything and had done so with both men and women, but no one called her a lesbian or gay. Crazy, but not gay.

Despite all this bitterness in Liza's life, all the unfairness that clung to her, she always managed to be positive. She wasn't false-perky. She wasn't someone who always looked on the bright side of life even when there wasn't one. Rather, she was the kind of person who believed that things would get better, that "this too shall pass." This attitude drove her brother Dave crazy, because he never quite got the best of her, no matter what he tried. She'd just shrug off his antics and move on.

It was this unyielding hope, this strident will, that Gwen loved about Liza. It kept them together long after Gwen's random attention should have wandered off. Liza was the lamppost and Gwen the moth, and for the years they lived together, Liza was happier than she'd ever been before.

This all changed in 1997 when a twenty-two year old Liza, under Gwen's insistent nudging, left their hometown to meet her idol, the Paragon. Some people are gifted, they fall in the 3rd percentile of human ability, but there are some that are statistical outliers, people with abilities that are beyond what we typically think of as human ability. Paragon was an outlier among outliers. From the time she was twelve, when she watched a video in class on the impact of outliers on history, she had maintained a vibrant crush on the hero Paragon. He stood out, not just because he was a living legend, but because he had a smile that made her toes curl. For her thirteenth birthday, her mother had bought her the only gift she'd ever liked that wasn't a book: a poster of the Paragon lifting a new Ford Mustang above his head with two bikini models draped over the hood. She hung the poster above her bed and memorized his every muscle. Every time he was on the news, she watched. This was about the only time she bothered to watch television, preferring to have her nose in a book instead. She read every interview on him and kept a secret scrapbook of his pictures clipped from magazines and newspapers. She wrote in her journal all of the amazing things she learned about the Paragon. He was heroically strong, he could bounce bullets off his chest, he could fly, and he never had a mean thing to say about anyone. He was larger than life in every way, and according to the gossip magazines, he was aggressively single. She wrote stories in her journal about the ways she would fix that, but she knew she'd never meet him. He only went to important places. He would fly to disaster zones trouble spots - wherever the UN or America needed him - and that was never Ohio. Liza kept a map of the world with little Xs on it to indicate a Paragon visit. To date, he'd only been in the state once to help out after a bunch of tornados had ripped up some tiny place to the southeast called Xenia. This weekend, the superhero drought changed. The Paragon had written his autobiography and was promoting it across the country, and he was going to be in person just a few hundred miles away in a mall bookstore in the big city. All she had to do was get there.

To be fair, Columbus was not considered a big city by many. It had a few modest skyscrapers, but the streets were hardly urban; it was more like a suburb that had gotten a little too big for its britches. Yet compared to Clarksdale and its two-traffic-light main street, Columbus was a veritable Mecca of steel and concrete complete with theaters, drugs not brewed in a trailer, and parades so long that they didn't really end; you just got tired of watching them and headed home. The grounds for the state fair were larger than the Clarksdale city limits, and when OSU's Buckeyes played, the tailgating population was triple Clarksdale's at the height of the post-war baby boom. To Liza, Columbus might as well have been a foreign country. Her little college was actually a satellite campus of Ohio State University, but she'd never been to the main campus before. She had been to the city only once, to see the zoo on a school field trip when she was eleven. All she could remember was that the bus smelled of plastic and motor oil, and that the zoo in the rain smelled worse.

At normal freeway speeds, the city was over two hours away, but along country roads that no one bothered with unless they were tending their fields or wanted to race their cars, it was only an hour or so. It felt like three as Liza white knuckled the dashboard while her brother drove at maniac speeds. She hadn't spoken to him or seen him in months, but all it took was an offer to pay for gas and beer and he was all too willing to visit his classmate who had already gone ahead to OSU. Dave drove an old Chevy Nova that despite being an antique could reach double the posted speed limit, which he often did. The car had belonged to their dad who used to endlessly tinker with it before he had run off with a waitress not much older than Liza. Dave carried on the tradition, keeping the old girl humming nicely while he picked up girls too young to be dating him.

Before the signing there was going to be events going on all day, and they started first thing in the morning. A parade, fireworks, an exhibition of local heroes, and a street festival, but the Paragon was only flying in for the book signing and wouldn't be a part of any of that.

Liza wanted to see it all, but she would miss most of it because she had failed to talk her brother into leaving any sooner then "whenever he damn well felt like". The plan he had agreed to, after much begging, was to drop her off at 2 PM and return at 1 AM. She would have to kill a lot time while David partied, and she risked riding home with a drunk brother, but she didn't really have a choice in the matter. She had a few books with her and had looked up some late-hour coffee places that catered to students, so she'd be fine. The bigger problem with asking Dave for a ride was that he wouldn't take her all the way downtown. He had agreed, barely, to drop her at the campus entrance. When he did drop her off, as soon as the door shut he roared off without a word.

Liza had worked out the bus route using old maps at the library, not realizing how big a city can be. What she thought was a short walk to pick up her bus was in fact a long walk across the huge campus and then down a few city blocks in an unforgiving wind. She passed more strangers than she'd ever seen in her life, and her heart didn't stop pounding until she found the bus stop and was safely in her seat on the bus.

The bus was surprisingly clean and devoid of passengers, which Liza appreciated, but it seemed intent on stopping at every intersection to pick up no one, and it wound through a ghetto of cramped student housing and run-down neighborhoods that made her shiver. Liza buried her head in a book and chewed on her thumbnail. She had a gas station map marked with the location of the Columbus City Center among the downtown buildings, and she occasionally looked out the window to see if she could make sense of the city from her map, but she couldn't.

The book she was reading was the Paragon's unofficial biography. Half of it was full of useless trivia that had little to do with the Paragon himself. Liza didn't mind. She read that some estimates placed the population of people with outliers at at one in a million depending on the definition used for outlier abilities. The number made them sound rare, but the book quickly pointed out that with six billion people in the world, the total number was actually quite large. On the other hand, most outlier abilities were unremarkable compared to those of the Paragon. Some people are gifted, perfect pianists, mathematical geniuses, the outliers had stranger abilities like people that could walk on water - that sort of thing. The Paragon, on the other hand, could juggle cars, shrug off bullets, and fly. He was also another extremely rare type of human – drop-dead gorgeous. In picture after picture he had a body that looked as if it were sculpted by Michelangelo along with a jawline custom made for Hollywood.

Also, the current Paragon wasn't the first Paragon, he was the third person to use the name. The first Paragon appeared back in the forties. According to the book, each successive Paragon had passed on their abilities to someone they deemed worthy, though the book didn't say how it was done or what was the criteria used for being worthy.

The first official Paragon sighting had occurred just after the Nazi's unveiled the Übermensch in their devastating campaign against Poland. All of the Übermensch had terrifying abilities and their images were plastered onto Axis propaganda posters. The "ideal of man," they were called, "the perfection of the master race," each more deadly than a battalion of tanks. The first Paragon was sent on a series of covert missions to unbalance the Third Reich in preparation for the Normandy invasion and to take down the Übermensch, though there weren't any details as to what happened.

The book did reprint several large glossies of the beach storming. Paragon was out in front, bullets bouncing off his chest like raindrops on an umbrella. After that day, his image was on every recruitment and Allied pro-war poster. He remained a recruitment icon until he retired, just before the Korean conflict. He was the least handsome of the three Paragons, and his image was so stylized from the posters that few people recognized him in person when he was out of his uniform. They would recognize his red, white and blue fatigues, the big white star on his chest, and his odd short blue cape, but not his face. The book claimed his teeth were actually never white, despite the gleam always portrayed on his million-watt smile.

The second Paragon had shown up a few years after the first retired, but he stayed out of military action and actively denounced the Vietnam War. He didn't last long, and he hung up his cape to protest the Tet Offensive, which made him popular in the counterculture but derided everywhere else. He had long hair, grew a creepy straggly beard, and never looked right in his uniform, the same uniform that thousands of school kids wore for Halloween and was portrayed in cartoon form on their lunch boxes. The book documented several psychedelic and protest songs that referred to him, but Liza didn't recognize any of them. There was a picture of him smoking a hookah just before he disappeared from the public eye.

The third Paragon appeared publicly for the first time in that famous picture of him reporting for duty and shaking hands with President Nixon right at the start of Nixon's first term. The book recounted all the details about how Paragon had turned the tide on the Vietnam War during a Christmas counter-offensive, but Liza skipped over the gory details. At the end of the chapter the book postulated that winning the Vietnam War created the environment that led to the age of super-villains. The theory goes that the Chinese and the Russians both paid for and supported these madmen during the Cold War as a way to counter America's newfound strength in Asia. True or not, the powered conflicts in the Third World, particularly the one in Nicaragua, directly led to the STOP treaties that banned outliers from active combat duty in all nations. But like the START talks on nuclear weapons, the STOP treaties didn't really change anything.

After the Berlin wall fell, the Paragon changed jobs at the insistence of President Reagan in order to head up the United Nations Task Force on Environmental Crisis Management, which most people knew only by their nickname, the Storm Busters. Hurricanes, earthquakes, volcanoes, floods, mudslides, and anything else Mother Nature would pitch at the world, the Storm Busters took on with Paragon in the lead. The ascension of the United States to dominance of the United Nations was directly credited to the Paragon.

The unofficial biography said so many nice things about the Paragon that Liza wondered what needed to be set straight in an official autobiography. She would find out soon enough. It was the official autobiography that the Paragon was signing today.

Aside from seasonal tornadoes, Ohio was not known for natural disasters, which meant the Paragon was seldom seen in the state outside of election years, so this event was a big deal for his fans. Only three hundred people would be let into the book signing. Advance tickets were sold by phone and had sold out in minutes. Gwen had spent a fortune with a scalper to buy the ticket Liza now clutched. They'd be eating Ramen for months. Every time she looked at the ticket, Liza hummed the golden ticket song from *Willy Wonka and the Chocolate Factory* and made a silly grin.

Then she looked up and saw they had turned right when they should have turned left. She got out of her seat and looked out the window on the other side and saw orange barrels blocking off the street. Construction signs proclaimed that the bridge was closed. In a panic she looked around the bus and finally noticed the taped-up signs showing the changed route.

Her heart sank. She'd picked a bus route that doesn't go downtown anymore.

2

Liza scanned the map on the wall trying to decode the route changes. Her heart was now pounding and it made it difficult for her to read clearly. She took a deep breath and stilled herself and read again. She needed to take a connection at the spots marked in red. Of course they'd just passed the last one. She pleaded with the driver for help. He'd obviously put up with this before, and he perfunctorily gave her a transfer slip to the connection that would take her downtown, but then he gave her a second to ride this same bus route back when the north bound bus came through. He dropped her off on a windy stop in front of a dingy bar covered in graffiti. It would be fifteen minutes for the northbound to come by, another ten to get back to the connection stop, another twenty minutes for the connection to arrive, and then she'd be headed the right way. All told, she estimated she'd be at least an hour later than she needed to be. She hugged herself in the bar's doorway, stomped her feet to keep warm, and cursed her brother between grinding teeth.

Several connections later, when she stepped off the last bus, she saw a sea of humanity. The streets were closed off for an entire block, and there were food vendors and various merchants in tiny tent pavilions lining the streets with endless crowds between them. Music blared from several directions, and someone was announcing things from a staticy loudspeaker. She couldn't make out a word. She tried to find the mall entrance and held her breath as she waded through the crowds like a salmon heading upstream. A new mother with a baby in a sling saw her confused look and took the time to point out the right way. For a brief moment she was happy for a dose of kindness in the impersonal swell of chaos, but that feeling faded as she entered the Columbus City Center mall and found it was three floors tall. The kiosk listed 144 different storefronts, and she was overwhelmed. There was a food court and fountains at the bottom, glass elevators running up the center, crosswalks at each level, escalators scrolling between levels, and dozens of shops swirling around each level's edge. It was so much to take in, and she had no idea what to do next. She knew she had to go down to the bottom, so she focused on the quickest way to do that. The elevator seemed to move too slowly, so she headed for the nearest escalator. She wanted to run down it, but too many people were in the way. Her foot beat nervously as the escalator slowly lowered her to the next level. At the end of it, she picked up her sneakers out of fear her laces would get chomped, and then she had to run around to the other side of the mall to go down another level.

There was music by a live band blasting throughout the mall that sounded awful. She vaguely knew the singer from some endlessly playing MTV video. She passed kids in Paragon costumes or carrying Paragon balloons and guys in Paragon t-shirts, and it made her smile to be among fellow fans. On the last escalator down, she decided there were more people in this mall than she'd met in her entire life, or maybe more than lived in her whole town. She gasped like she needed an inhaler, something she hadn't needed for years. She gulped air and started to experience an infuriating case of hiccups.

She reached the bottom, and it was clear where the bookstore was because security guards had it roped off and hundreds of people were begging to get in. She worked her way forward until she could see through the store's glass walls. Inside were rows upon rows of black folding chairs all filled up with waiting people. The doors were closed when Liza shoved her way up to them. She had to shout above all the noise that she needed to get in, but the rent-a-cops didn't hear her over the crowd. She waved her book and ticket over her head to get their attention and some nearby high school girls saw the ticket and started squealing and pointing. People started to grab at the ticket, and Liza clutched it tightly to her chest. The security guards sensed a riot and started asking everyone to get back while one dark-skinned guard took her by the shoulders and escorted her into the bookstore.

Unbelievably, inside the bookstore it was louder. All of the girls and their moms and the occasional male fan were yelling or chanting cheers, and in the enclosed space the sound echoed like a thunderstorm. The books didn't absorb much of the noise, especially since most of them had been moved away to make room for the crowd.

After checking her ticket twice, the security guard sat her down in the last empty seat in the back, right next to the emergency exit.

Fortunately, the Paragon was an hour late as well. Unfortunately, this made the crowd unruly to the point that self-important moms were berating the bookstore staff. The commotion made the guards, both inside and outside of the bookstore, nervous. Liza looked again at the guards. They weren't mall cops or hired security, though there were some of those outside. These guards all wore black suits with earpieces like the Secret Service or the FBI did in the movies. There were several of them at the exit in the back, and she tried to look at them out of the corner of her eye because they made her nervous. She decided they were all watching the crowd like Gwen's cat would stalk a sunbeam: necks craned, bodies tensed, legs arched and ready to pounce. They were making her nervous. She finally stared at the badge one of them had on, which had his photo in a clear plastic case clipped to his belt, and it read UNSD. She had no idea what a UNSD was. She discovered that in addition to the earpieces, they had throat mics that allowed them to mumble but apparently still be heard by each other. It was odd watching them talk; it was like watching a ventriloquist next to his dummy. She eventually realized they weren't watching the crowd at all. They were searching for something specific. She started to wonder what they could be worried about when the speakers inside and outside started blasting the Star Spangled Banner.

He was here.

Every head, inside and out, bent in the same direction as the Paragon flew in. He spiraled down from the ceiling and began looping in huge arcs that brought him even with the walkways at each of the mall's levels. As he past each level, he held out his hand and high-fived anyone who leaned out with their hand. He was even quick enough to fist bump a few people. He was taking his time, and the cheers were deafening.

This Paragon has his own look, he never wore the uniform the first two Paragons wore, and Liza recalled watching him tell Johnny Carson how much he hated the cape. Instead, he wore his now-classic skintight red shirt, loose denim blue pants, and his signature red-dyed snakeskin cowboy boots. Emblazoned on his chest was the giant white star logo that all of the Paragons had worn.

Paragon the first had worn his sewn onto his fatigues, and Paragon the second had worn it on the shoulders of his sleeves. This Paragon's star was on his chest, and it glowed in the dark.

He landed gently, but with a flourish, outside the store. The security detail had cleared the way for his landing and opened the door for him. Camera flashes went off like sparklers and girls of all ages waved things for him to sign as they screamed in pitches that could break glass. Paragon just ignored them all with a wave and walked inside. When the doors closed behind him, the people on the outside pressed up against the glass. Liza heard the music outside fade out, but with the screaming and cheering both inside and outside, it didn't get any quieter. Liza had never heard anything like it before, even at homecoming when her brother played on the varsity team. She thought back to the way David described Ohio State games or the way Gwenifer described rock concerts she went to. This had to be worse. Liza, feeling claustrophobic in the small space with so many people, clutched the edges of her chair. She wanted to run outside and find the largest empty space she could find and just shiver.

"Hello, Cleveland!" roared the Paragon as he walked up a security-enforced, red-carpeted aisle to the microphone on the tiny stage.

"It's Columbus," some brave soul yelled out as the Paragon adjusted the height of the mike.

"Whatever," he replied from blaring speakers that projected outside as well. "It's good to be out in the Midwest, America's breadbasket. You're the good people whose backs support this great country, and it's an honor to be among such heroes." He sounded a bit snarky and cheesy to Liza, like a comedian working a room, but the crowd ate it up and roared even louder in rapture.

"So," he said with a perfect smile full of perfect teeth, "anybody here buy my book?"

A sea of arms shot up waving copies.

"Well for those who didn't, I'm told this fine little establishment can help you out, isn't that right Mr. Brooks?" The Paragon pointed to the nervous store manager who gulped and tried to shrink and hide in plain sight, only to fail miserably.

"And best of all," the Paragon winked, "I've pre-signed every one of them. Now unfortunately my duties have me leaving you all earlier than planned, so there won't be time for any personal signings, but the kindly Mr. Brooks has two boxes of signed copies, and not only have I arranged a nice discount for all of you, but you all get a first shot at buying them before they go on sale to the general public. You're so lucky." He winked yet again.

Screams of joy filled the room, although a few pulled out their purses and pocketbooks to calculate if they had enough for an unplanned purchase. Liza didn't check. She barely had enough money for the bus fare back.

"I do have time for a few questions," the Paragon said, his finger sweeping the room. "Who'd like to go first?"

He pointed to a chesty woman in the first row who blurted out, "Who was your first love?"

The Paragon shook his head. "That's in the book. You'll have to read it and find out. Next?"

"What's your real name?" a mom asked, cutting off her daughter who had been pointed to.

"Sorry. Confidential. But my friends call me Awesome. Next question?" People were all standing and waving for attention. Liza stood on her wobbling chair to see over them, but she wasn't having any luck because she was so far in the back.

"What's the scariest thing you've ever done?"

"You mean other than face a room of screaming women undressing me with their eyes?"

Liza sat down. "He sounds like my brother. A total conceited jerk."

"Next question," the Paragon said as he levitated slightly off the floor. The room to cried, "Ooooh," in unison.

"Is it true you don't need to eat?"

"Only when the service is less than four stars. Next?"

"How do you hold someone without…I mean…well, without breaking them?"

"Carefully. And for someone as lovely as you I'd always be careful. Time for a few more. Next?"

Liza looked at her watch: barely fifteen minutes. The Paragon had turned a city upside down, and Liza had jumped through a dozen flaming hoops to see him, and this was all he was giving the city?

"If you're indestructible, how do you cut your hair or shave?"

"I'm not indestructible, just really tough," he said winking and running a hand over his buzz cut head of blond hair. "And that's a personal secret, one that I'm going to reveal in my next book, *The Complex Life of Being Special*, and I can tell you now I've just inked the contract so the book should be out by Christmas." Lots of murmuring and approval in the crowd. "Last question."

"Unt vat vould you do iv you vere nothink? Ja? Just a normal, liken das rest ov us? Ja?"

The crowd went silent as the Paragon looked around for the speaker, but the voice came from all around, a man's raspy voice oozing out of the sound system. The security guards became agitated, and then all at once they clutched their ears in pain and fell over as one with a dramatic *thump*.

Paragon spit out the words "Dr. Psi."

Confusion and panic, verging on hysteria, washed over the crowd as necks strained to look where the Paragon was now focused. They looked at Liza, or rather directly behind her. Liza yelped as she felt an arm around her neck, pulling her out of her chair and making her stand. She felt the bite of a razor against her neck. She clenched her hands when she felt the burn from a nick on her throat.

"Be a gut girl, ja? Do not moof," said the frail voice in her ear. "Iv you moof, you vill die. Understand? Zere vill be much blud. Is not beink so easy to get sie blud from clothink. I should know. Unt I vish to afoid zis."

The Paragon left the podium and walked up the carpeted aisle between the chairs, slowly but deliberately, as the crowd froze in shock. "Let her go, Psi. This is between you and me."

"Jess. Jess it is."

Liza didn't move, but from the corner of her eye, she saw her captor, clad in a dingy old lab coat that needed cleaning, raise a gun-shaped device clutched in his frail hand. The hair on her neck and arms stood up as the weapon began to hum. Spirals of blue and white light energy arced along the translucent shell of its barrel. The muzzle ended in a large cone where light raced about and then coalesced into a glowing ball that began to fill the cone.

"There are innocent people here, Psi. We know how this ends, with you behind bars, but if you harm any of these people, there will be no mercy for you," Paragon said wagging his finger at him as if he were scolding a child.

"Zen I von't harm zem. Only you." Dr. Psi pulled the trigger and at the same time clutched Liza tightly against him. The knife nicked her again, and she could feel the blood running down her neck. Then her eyes were assaulted by the brilliant blaze of the beam that shot out of the weapon. The beam struck the Paragon in the center of his chest, and even though he'd braced himself against a strong force, he went limp when it hit. He fell to the ground like a rag doll that had been let drop. Dr. Psi kept the beam focused on him, not letting up after he hit the ground. "Is vorkink! Vho has sie last vord, eh? Me! I am ze vun! My positron ray iz scramblink sie synapses in jour cortex, prefenting neurons vrom communicatink, disruptink all electrochemical communication! Jour body iz not jour own. Sie stench risink up is not jour ego, it iz jour bovels relaxink! Sie muscle's vill to keep zem clenched iz gone! HA! But jou can not hear me, or see me, or zink ov anythink at all. I haf beaten jou, unt all zee vorld vill see it!"

The maniac's speech was being broadcast across all the sound systems in the bookstore and the mall, and everyone was silent in shocked response.

"Ach. Sie immobilizink jou vas not my goal Herr Paragon. Nein. I haf somethink verse in mind." Liza choked as one of his hands stretched to push a button on the weapon. The weapon sent a new pulse of blue light spiraling around the original white beam. "Zis carrier wave, ja? It iz cycling at ze delta vrequency generated by das REM sleep. It iz stimulating sie cells ov jour brain, harmonizink zem. Zen iv I flip sie final svitch…? Vell, vhy giff avay my secret vhen I can show jou?"

Liza didn't know what came over her. She was terrified, overwhelmed, bleeding, and pounded by a tsunami of adrenalin. She took the huge autobiography in her hands and swung it over her head and smacked the madman in the face. He staggered back, clutching his nose at the same moment he pushed the last button. The weapon sent out a second blue beam spiraling in a counter direction to the first and thus making a double helix of blue lighting around a core of iridescent white. Liza felt the hand pull away from her neck as the doctor clutched his face, so she turned and hit him again with the book. He was older than she thought, a frail wispy thing in his 80's or 90's, and he was no match for her. He instinctively covered his face with both hands and dropped the weapon. Still firing, it bounced on the ground and caught her leg in its beam. Liza's eyes exploded with color as if a flashbulb had gone off in them, and she was left lightheaded and dizzy. Then she had the sensation she was floating outside of her body, as if she were flying in a dream. The colors faded to be replaced with featureless white light in all directions. There was no sound, and she felt numb.

She was sure this was the end, that she was dying. She wondered why her life wasn't flashing before her eyes. Then everything went black.

3

The migraine pressure trying to squeeze out between Liza's eyes forced her awake, leaving her with a drilling pain in her forehead and a shrill ringing in her ears. Her eyelids felt heavy, as if they'd been taped closed, but by some concerted willpower she got them to slowly open. Once opened she discovered she needn't have bothered, the room was too dark to see anything at all. She turned her head slightly, and her brain felt as if it were swinging on a tire swing, so she tried not to move. She'd had a hangover almost this bad once, on her twenty-first birthday. On that day she had decided to celebrate and had let Gwenifer mix the drinks. A mistake she never repeated.

Liza could sense her arms and legs, but they wouldn't move on command. This made her heart race in panic, which made the pounding of the migraine worse. She tried to move every which way she could think of, wiggle fingers and toes, wrists, ankles and hips, but nothing happened. She became aware of something around her throat as she swallowed heavily. It was a neck brace, she was sure of it.

The adrenalin really kicked in and fireworks of phantom light flashed in rhythm to the pain behind her eyes. She tried to calm herself by breathing slowly and by paying attention to any detail she could make out to distract her thoughts. There was a bed beneath her or something softer than the ground. There was a faint blinking light in the dark in the corner of her eye. She turned her eyes slowly to avoid the spinning feeling and saw more lights blinking and thought she heard humming around the ringing in her ears. "Medical equipment," she guessed. "I'm in a hospital?" She could feel the slight tug of something on her arms. Restraints?

Questions bubbled up at once. "Does my family know I'm here? Where is everyone? Where are the nurses and doctors? How did I get here? How bad off am I?"

A brilliant ball of flame flicked on overhead as if the sun had suddenly risen above her. The flash brought with it an onslaught of color spots swirling before her eyes which mixed into a nausea that hit her in a gut-wrenching wave. When she tried to retch, she discovered there was something in her throat. Her lips and tongue were held back by a breathing tube, and her eyes and brow went wide as she wondered how she could not have noticed that. Of course, now that she did notice it, she felt herself wanting to gag non-stop. There was a shadow over her eyes that momentarily dimmed the blinding glare overhead. She heard a voice, but it sounded as if it were down a long corridor and underwater. The shadow, however, suggested the voice was really next to her. Liza thought it was a woman, but she couldn't make out the words. She vaguely felt hands touch her body and face and smelled something sweet like bubblegum before her thoughts became too heavy to lift and she fell back to sleep.

When Liza awoke again, her throat was sore and she eventually realized the tube was out of her mouth. The lights were on, but dimmed. She could see, but it was all gauzy and fuzzy, like a Vaseline-coated camera lens. Liza looked around and found she could move her head now; the dizziness remained, but the restraining collar was gone. The migraine had, thankfully, dulled to a throbbing ache, but persisted in its annoyance. Her mouth was dry, and in general she felt weak and drained.

A doctor appeared in her field of view, and she wanted to jump in surprise, but her body was still not responding as it should. Her sense of touch was telling her that her wrists were restrained, as were her ankles, but she should have been able to move some, and her body seemed to have no interest in obeying.

"You had us scared there for a while, old man! Good to see you come around, Colonel," said the doctor as he scanned the vitals on the chart.

"Wug grh," Liza gurgled.

"You need to just relax, Colonel. Don't try to talk or move. You've been through a hell of a trauma. Like nothing we've ever seen before. But your vitals are good, and from what we can tell, the side effects are minimal and receding. My guess is you'll be up and about in a few days. At least that's my pick in the floor pool, and I intend to collect! But for now just rest." The doctor sounded jovial, but Liza was sure it was an act to make her fell better. It failed.

The doctor put some ice chips on Liza's tongue, and they tasted crisp and metallic and delightfully wet as the water rolled down her throat. "I think we can get rid of these now," he said as he fumbled with something that sounded alternately like metal and the shredding rip of Velcro. Liza's arms felt lighter, as if they were floating next to her. One hand, her left, seemed to move on its own, drifting across her body, and then it felt cold. She looked and saw that a tray had been slid over across her lap, and her hand was now holding a cup of ice on the tray. There was something wrong. Her hand looked freakishly large. Badly swollen? The fingers were fat and long, the skin rough. Her eyes went wide and she started to sit up, but the doctor gently pushed her back down. "I don't want to give you any more sedatives. They don't work well on you, and you've already had more than would be healthy for a normal person. I need you to relax. Let your amazing body recover on its own."

Liza looked into the doctor's face. He was Indian with dark caramel skin and a razor-thin beard and very short, curly, black hair. His cheekbones were sharp, but his brown eyes were soft, and he had a velvety voice. Her heart pounded a bit, and she felt her face flush. He was gorgeous, and she thought a few quick naughty thoughts about being examined by him, which made her blush. She pushed the thoughts away, but decided if she was capable of being horny, she was going to be ok. That one normal feeling in all this oddness made her more comfortable, and she genuinely relaxed. "Ugh kay. Grrest." Liza fell back to sleep.

The third time Liza woke, she felt fine. So fine that she kept mentally inventorying herself before moving to make sure she was fine. No nausea, no headache; her limbs felt normal, and she could move them. When she opened her eyes, the light was bright, but she could see normally. The ringing in her ears was gone, and she could make out the humming and beeping of the medical equipment around her, as well as the distant sounds of nurses moving about the ward and the hospital activity beyond her room. She hadn't been in many hospitals before; her family couldn't afford them. She had gone to urgent care centers or free clinics, but she'd broken her arm once falling off her bike, and memories of that time now came flooding back. Instinctively, she flexed her arm and, with the opposite hand, felt the forearm where the break had been. There was no break of course, but there was a thick muscular arm with way more hair than it should have had. She looked down at her hands and arms and discovered they remained grossly oversized and swollen and oddly covered in black hair. They looked like a man's arms and hands. Her heart skipped a beat, and she pulled away the sheets to expose her man-sized feet wiggling in the air. Her mind was occupied by one single thought.

"Shit."

She touched her chest and instead of an ample bosom, she found rock hard muscle and a thick patch of hair. She lifted up the sheets into the air, and as they billowed out, she looked down the length of her naked body and saw a very hairy male body complete with a – she slammed the sheets back down as her eyes bulged.

"*Ahhhhh!*" Liza screamed.

Nurses of both genders rushed in, followed by her doctor, who was unwinding a stethoscope from his neck. They simultaneously asked what was wrong and tried to calm her down as she kept screaming. The doctor pushed his way through to her and shoved her shoulders back down. "You must relax, please, Colonel!"

"*Mirror!*" Liza roared. "*Now!*"

The doctor waved to one of the nurses who complied by rummaging around and producing a hand-held mirror, which the doctor placed in Liza's hand. She slowly brought it up to her face with her left hand and touched her cheek with the other. In the mirror she saw the Paragon touching his cheek. "Oh God! What's happened to me!"

"You're fine. Please calm down." Machines began bleating in distress. "I've explained to you before, Colonel.

You suffered a very traumatic event. You may feel a bit disoriented, but that will pass."

"Who am I?" asked Liza as she stared down at the doctor. "What's my name?"

The doctor took out a small penlight and flashed it back and forth in Liza's eyes, then made a note on his tablet. "You may be suffering from some short term memory issues or severe disassociation. This happens with some traumas. It will fade, I promise. You are Colonel John West. You've been unconscious for several days."

"Days!"

"Yes. But don't worry. Control has been in to see you many times. Everything is being taken care of."

"Control? What the hell is Control? What is happening to me!"

The doctor turned and consulted quietly with the nurses and another doctor who had shown up unannounced. Liza then noticed the men in black suits that were stationed at the edges of the room. Three of them. Same as the men at the bookstore. They all stared at her intently. She felt very naked and exposed and pulled the sheets up to her chin and shivered.

The doctor made like a schoolteacher at recess and herded everyone out of the room. Even the men in black retreated to just outside the doorway. The doctor returned alone. "The shock you're experiencing is more than we expected, and we need to reduce sensory stimulation. I'm also going to order up a full battery of psychological tests to better assess your condition. These will include personality tests, memory tests, and cognitive assessments. We'll get to the bottom of this and develop a regimen to get you back into perfect form. You have my word."

He held out his hand for a handshake, and Liza hesitantly snuck her freakishly large man hand from beneath the covers and used it to shake his hand.

Apparently she squeezed too hard because she heard a knuckle cracking sound, and the doctor yanked his hand away and held it cursing under his breath. "For now, I think you need to rest. I'll return in an hour with Doctor Sampson, and we can begin the testing. I think I'll also schedule you for another MRI, but it's unlikely to show much given your unique physiology. We might try an EEG on a very high sensitivity."

Liza poked her head out from under the covers. "Doctor? Um," she read his badge, "Sure-ish?"

"Anjai Suresh. I introduced myself earlier, but you've been experiencing some short-term memory loss. This is actually the tenth time you've woken up." He showed Liza his ID badge clipped to his smock. "I'm a paraphysiologist from the Cleveland Clinic, and you're probably not aware of it, but I've consulted with your team's physician several times in the past, and I've spoken directly to him twice this morning." He gestured out into the ward beyond the room. "Some of Mount Carmel's attending staff are actually mine and flew down with me. The rest are locals, but I've cleared them all with your UNSAD Agents. You're in good, safe, care."

"Doctor Suresh, were there any other... um victims? Anyone else hurt?"

"There was a stampede of people, but fortunately the injuries were all superficial. All of them have been released at this point."

"Nothing more serious?" Liza realized that her voice sounded different too, deep like a man's.

"Some of the UNSAD Agents suffered some temporary hearing damage due to the sonic pulse directed through their headsets, but all have recovered their hearing within acceptable OSHA standards for construction work."

"Was there a girl? A young woman? About four foot seven, heavy set, dark hair?"

Suresh flipped screens with quick swipes on his tablet. "Yes, there was. She was treated for lacerations to her throat, and some minor head trauma, likely a concussion from falling. We kept her for observation, and she was released yesterday into police custody."

"Police?"

"For interrogation. I believe they suspected her of colluding with Doctor Psi."

Liza sat up and shoved the covers down. "That's ridiculous!"

Suresh stepped back a bit. "I'm not at liberty to judge one way or the other. I'm only your personal physician. And that was pure speculation on my part. I'm sure I have no idea what they want with her beyond her being a material witness."

"Material witness?"

"If this is an important matter, I can allow you to speak to one of your UNSAD Agents to follow up, because I am *not* qualified. But I *am* going to limit the duration of the contact. I do not want you agitated. Your best chance for recovery is rest."

"I'd like to speak to her." Liza noticed the doctor's unease, and an idea struck her. "Um… that's an order."

"Colonel, I don't approve…" The doctor swallowed loudly to cover the fear in his voice.

"I said, that's an order!"

"I have the authority when you are in this state to-" His voice was wavering though, lacking confidence, like her mom sounded when she was grounding her.

"Now! Lives could depend on it!"

"I'll see what I can do, Colonel." He tapped on his screen and then looked up and saluted. "Sir."

He looked like a stricken puppy, and Liza felt guilty. "Sorry I yelled. It's just very very important to me. I need you to bring her here. As soon as you can. Okay? Please?"

"You MUST be injured if you're saying please," Suresh muttered, but he stopped arguing and completed his physical exam in silence save for the necessary chatter. Liza tried not to freak out about being touched or by the strange sensations with which her body responded. When Suresh finally left, she hugged herself and shivered.

When she thought no one was looking, she got out of bed. There was a gown hanging up that went on backward so that it tied in the back, and she found it awkward to tie when she tried to put it on. Her large long arms reached around well enough, but they were clumsy to operate. She kept underestimating her movements and ultimately ripped off one of the ties with her newfound and unexpected strength. She discovered she was also affixed with little white circles of tape and wires that led to machines that beeped loudly when she pulled the circles off. Almost immediately, a nurse came in, appearing in response to the sound. "I'm going to the bathroom," Liza barked, and the nurse stopped dead in her tracks, even backed up a bit. "Is that ok with you?" The nurse nodded and backed out of the room, turning on the light to the attached bathroom on her hurried way out.

Liza shambled to the bathroom, moving like a clumsy zombie. The agents were watching her from outside the room, so she slammed the door. She did it a bit too hard. The floor shook and a thunderclap rang out across the entire ward. Inside the bathroom Liza shivered some more and willed herself to look into the mirror and saw the Paragon's face grimacing back at her. A pang in her abdomen told her she really did have to pee. She'd been lying to get some privacy, but now that the thought was in her head, the need to go was urgent.

34

She fumbled to get the lid up and the gown out of the way so she could sit on the cold seat. She had to adjust and shuffle around and widen her legs to get the foreign penis pointed in the right direction without her having to touch it. Then she put her fingers in her ears to block the sound as she peed. When she was done, she wondered what to do and decided to wipe up with toilet paper wrapped around her hands. Even though she tried not to touch it, it seemed to move on its own. She didn't know it could do that. She'd never seen one long enough to know anything useful about it.

A part of her mind recalled how many times she'd fantasized about this body, but touching it like this just felt criminal. Or rather she thought it was criminal, but her body seemed to have a mind of its own. As the memories of her own arousal came to mind, the body began to be physically aroused. "*Stop that!*" she yelled at it, and soaked a towel in cold water from the sink and shoved the towel onto her groin. The cold was horribly unpleasant, but it worked to kill the erection before it fully formed.

There was a knock on the bathroom door. "Are you alright, Colonel?"

"Fine!" Liza squeaked. "I'm fine." She held her breath until she was certain the person had left. She put the seat down and sat on the toilet. She looked at the hair on her arms. "Where did all of this come from? He's not this hairy in the posters. Do they airbrush him, like a centerfold?"

She put her elbows on her knees and her chin in her hands. "What the hell am I gonna do? I don't want to be a boy! They smell!" She sniffed her own armpits and was hit by a smashing blow of acrid stench. "Ugh! I do smell!"

She was silent and still in the bathroom, deep in thought, leaned over with elbows on her thighs, chin in her hands. A half hour slipped past, then, as if a gun went off, she sat up straight. "Wait. If I'm him, I'm not just strong. I can fly!" She looked around to see if anyone was watching, then mentally yelled at herself for being an idiot since she was still in the bathroom with the door closed.

She stood up and put her arms to her sides, then shook them out and let them hang loose. She brought her feet together, then decided they should be apart, and then pulled them together again. "So how do I fly? I just think up? Do I jump?" A feeling of lightness came over her and, fearing a dizzy spell, she shot out a hand to catch the sink edge. The corner of it shattered in her hand. "I think I'll wait until I'm outside to try flying. No flying," she said, and she felt her weight return.

She checked herself in the mirror again and then made a few faces, watching the foreign features respond correctly, but a little differently than she expected. Her smirk looked creepy, and her smile was way too exaggerated. "Different face muscles and shape," she guessed. "How did this happen? Didn't that crazy guy say he wanted the Paragon's body or something? It must have worked, but it happened to me instead. *Oh!* Is the old guy inside my body? *Eww!* Or is the Paragon in my body? Am I in my body? Am I a copy? How does this work?!"

She looked at her teeth and tongue and nose as she thought, "Not Paragon. John. John West. I have the body of Colonel John West, the Paragon. I wonder if that's a secret? What will they do with me once they find out I know his name? Can I be arrested for impersonating an officer?" Her face went white and blank. "Oh no. If I've been here for days then I missed my final!"

Another knock on the door. "Colonel. You have a visitor."

"Just a minute!" Liza flushed and washed her hands and checked that her robe was on and covering everything important. She decided it wasn't staying on well enough, so she gripped it closed with one hand behind her back. "Ok. I'm coming out." She fumbled with the lever, bending it a bit before pushing it down to open the door.

As Liza shuffled out into the room, she saw her own body standing before her in an orange jumpsuit, hands cuffed with plastic zip ties. There was a large white bandage taped onto her throat. On either side of her was an agent. Liza, the body, was staring daggers at her. The agent on the left asked, "Is this the person of interest Colonel? We haven't gotten a word out of her yet. She claimed Fifth Amendment rights and hasn't said a word since."

"Uh yeah. Yeah, that's her. What has she, uh, done?"

The agent on the right, an African-American with a wonderfully smooth voice that would have made Liza's toes tingle if they were her own toes, said, "She hasn't done anything that we know of. Security footage has her situated in exactly the place where Dr. Psi appeared, and she was the last person to arrive for the book signing, and she went directly to the only open seat."

"She was also cut badly," Liza pointed out, "and you can't really call it a signing when the books were already signed." Liza put her hands on her hips, thought better of it, and crossed her arms.

"True," said the left agent. "But then she broke into a fight with several of our agents when we tried to help her up. She's been quite a handful."

Liza's body sneered.

The right agent added, "We can hold her for the assault charges, but that's all we have. The name she's given us is Elisabeth Lang. However her driver's license and tax records indicate that she is Liza Dunkirk. School records are mixed. Lang appears to be her mother's maiden name, while Dunkirk seems to be the surname of her estranged father. She's twenty-three and comes from a place called

Clarksdale, same state, just west of here. She's had a history of disciplinary problems in school and acquired several suspensions in response. She's also been arrested for vandalism."

"That's supposed to be sealed!"

The UNSAD Agents looked at her blankly.

"I mean, if she was a juvenile, those records would be sealed, right?"

Right laughed. "Yeah sure, sir. Now, her roommate is interesting. She has a history of drug use and several arrests, but all minor offenses."

Left added, "Troubled kids are always the easiest to recruit by terrorists. She has your poster over her bed and she's a member of your online fan club, so she has a little stalker action going on."

Liza's body raised an eyebrow.

"So," said Left, "we're suspicious there's a connection. We're still looking."

"She's innocent," barked Liza.

"Sir?" said Right.

"I saw her reactions when that Dr. Psi guy grabbed her. She wasn't acting. I think this is all just a big misunderstanding."

"Why did you want to see her then?" asked Left.

"I was worried. I wanted to make sure she was alright. I saw the…um…cut. It looked painful." Liza quickly added, "Not that I know what pain feels like since I'm indestructible and all. I just meant that it looked like it hurt her. I don't think she has any connection to the mad doctor. Her struggling actions probably saved me. She hit the Psi guy with a book. She's a hero. You can let her go."

"Colonel," said Right, "are you sure?"

"Totally."

Right scratched his chin. "We'll take that under advisement. She still has the assault charges to answer for, but given the chaotic circumstances, I think the charges can be dropped. Would that work, sir?"

"Yes! Yes. Yes, that would be good. Do that."

Liza's body grinned an evil grin.

"Um, my mind has blanked," said Liza. "Side effect of all this crazy stuff. I hate to be rude, but what are your names again?"

"Agent 33, sir," said Left, "and of course, Agent 34." He gestured to his right.

"We haven't been your field men for very long, sir, so don't feel bad," said Agent 34.

"I just meant your real names, not you're...uh...code names."

"We can't break that protocol, not in front of a civilian, sir!" Agent 33 said, nodding to Liza's body.

"Family protection act, Colonel. You're the only one who ignores it, sir, but respectfully we do not. I myself have a wife and two kids. I've got to protect them," said 34.

"Sorry. You're right. I know better. I was just thinking that we've known each other so long that it seems weird calling you 32 and 33."

"34," said 34. "We're 33 and 34. 32 was injured at the bookstore. He'll be on medical leave for another week, at least."

"At least," agreed 33.

Liza rubbed her temples where a new headache was forming. "Can you just go outside for a bit and let me talk to her alone? I think she'll open up to me."

"Woah woah, sir," said 34. "We can't release a prisoner into your custody while you're in an ICU."

Liza's brow furrowed and she frowned. "She's a tiny woman in handcuffs, and I'm the Paragon. Sick or not, I think I can handle her."

"He's got a very good point 34," said 33.

"Yeah, I suppose," said 34. "But we'll have to wait outside. And please keep it short, sir. Number 2 will have our heads for agreeing to this. I'd rather he not find out."

33 put his arm on 34's shoulder. "We can catch up with 27 and 28 outside. 28 had me for Secret Santa last year and I've been looking for an opportunity to have words with him. A snowman tie with blinking light eyes? Really."

There was some more minor chit chat along with some warnings to Liza's body, and then 33 and 34 left.

"About time," said Liza's body.

"Who are you?" Liza asked her body.

"Elisabeth Lang. Who else would I be?" said Liza's body.

"You are not Elisabeth. I am. And I never stand like that. I slouch. You're not slouching."

"Interesting."

"That's all you have to say? Interesting? Because I wouldn't say interesting. I'd say this is totally fucked up."

"If you tell them you're not the Paragon, they are going to lock you into a research ward and pick you apart to figure out what happened, and then they are going to lock you away as a security risk. You'll be treated like a spy. You don't want that."

"What I want is my body back, and you have it," said Liza, stomping on the floor for emphasis.

"Well I don't want mine back. I'm sick of the spotlight. This is an overdue vacation, and I'm going to take it."

"Are you really John West?"

Liza's body shifted uneasily. "How do you know that name? Can you read my memories?"

"You said *my* memories. So this is *your* body. You *are* the Paragon."

"Nope. I'm Elisabeth. You're the Paragon now. Have fun."

"Liza!"

"Liza what?"

"My name is Liza, not Elisabeth! Nobody calls me Elisabeth."

"Nobody calls me John. It's Paragon, or Colonel, or sir. Well, except for Cinaed, but she calls me Johnny boy."

"Fine, Johnny boy, we need to tell these number guys who we are. And the doctors, too. Let them fix it. You don't get to vacation in my body. I won't allow it."

"Yes, you will. Because if you don't, I'll tell them you're working for Dr. Psi. That you're his spy to learn all the secrets of the Sads."

"Sads?"

"Sads. The UNSAD? UN Special Actions Detail?" Liza looked at John blankly. John jerked his thumb to the door. "The guys in black outside."

"Oh." Liza looked at the room door. "So, Sads are what?"

"They're the human liaisons between the outliers and the United Nations. Actually NATO, but they do have to answer to the UN Security Council. The Chinese hate them. They're supposed to keep an eye on us, but in reality they do all the scut work for us. Crowd control and paperwork mostly. It's a lot of legal hell to be an outlier. Crappy job. We usually just call them Agents, but I call them 'sad' instead of UNSAD. They hate that."

Liza bit the nail of Paragon's thumb, her mental gears turning in slow clanks. "Why do you need a vacation? Why don't you want your body back?"

"Because it's like being a rat in a cage, or a monkey in a zoo."

"That doesn't tell me anything."

"You'll see. Besides. I kinda like your body. A little too pudgy and short for my tastes, but I do like these!" John West cupped the breasts on Liza's body and shook them and gave them a good squeeze.

"*Stop that!*" Liza yelled as her foot pounded the floor like a sledgehammer.

34 poked in his head. "Everything alright?"

"Yes!" Said Liza and John in unison.

"Leave my boobs alone," whispered Liza as loudly as she could.

"You get to fly, and lift cars over your head. I get to squeeze a few tits whenever I want. It's a fair trade," John said with a wolfish grin.

"*It is not.*" Liza said, her voice quivering, but not shouting, as she tried to be firm.

"Look," said John, "The only one who can switch us back is Dr. Psi because he made us this way, and from what I overheard, he got away in the confusion. Until we can find him, we're stuck like this. But, until then, no one needs to know. If anyone found out, my enemies would smell weakness and come after you in swarms. And not just you; they'd come after me in this body, and they'd come after your family."

"I can't be you! I can barely walk in this hulking monstrosity," Liza said, gesturing clumsily with John's body. "Let alone be a hero."

"And I don't know how to have multiple orgasms, but I intend to find out."

"*You are not having sex with my body!*" Liza yelled, and 33 and 34 came rushing in. They yanked John up by the shoulders.

"Got a little too mouthy to the boss there didja?" asked 33.

"Stop it," said Liza. "He was just being rude. I can handle this."

"He?" 33 and 34 said in unison.

"Paragon," John interrupted in a syrupy voice, "meant Dr. Psi. The doctor promised I could cuddle with the

Paragon when he was done making it a vegetable, so I went along with his plan."

"I knew it was something sick like that," said 34.

"But she didn't go through with it," interrupted Liza, "she tricked him and hit him at the last minute. She had no choice. Because… Because he said he'd kill everyone if she didn't cooperate. Yes. So she played along. And then… and then instead she signaled Paragon, I mean me, and then she bonked the creepy bad guy, thereby saving me and everyone else. She's a hero. *Just like I said.*" Liza was staring down John.

"Then what was the yelling about sex for?" asked 33.

"I wanted a little reward," John said, appearing to moon over Liza. "Can't blame a girl for trying can you? He's so dreamy."

Liza scowled. "Maybe we should lock him, I mean her, up for awhile."

John made doe eyes with Liza's face. "You wouldn't do that to your biggest fan would you? All I wanted was what anyone would want. A chance to be with you for a while. Just a short while. Then everything will go back to normal."

"Ok. Then fine," snorted Liza, "but there are a lot of things I've got to know first."

"You aren't seriously going to fool around with this kid," said 34 with a disgusted look.

"That's not what I meant," said Liza, "I'm going to drag *her* around my world for a day. Let her have a chance to wear *my* shoes. Show her the ropes, and *tell* her about my life. Then I'll take her home and she can show me around *her* world. So we get to *know each other*. Every fan's dream come true."

"I don't like the sound of any of this," said 33.

"Me neither," said 34. "Colonel, you're not yourself today."

"Oh but I love it," said John with a quick interruption, "that would make me so happy. Just give me a day. You won't regret it."

"I already do," said Liza.

4

Dr. Suresh returned and threw everyone out then ordered Liza back to bed. Liza fell instantly into an exhausted sleep.

John was questioned some more but eventually freed, and all charges were dropped, although 33 and 34 were assigned to escort him at all times when the Paragon wasn't. This meant babysitting him in a hotel room while he watched cable as Liza recovered. John had been given back Liza's clothes, but apparently couldn't get the bra on and decided to go without it. He was also having trouble walking in Liza's platform shoes and staggered about as best he could. 33 and 34 just griped under their breaths, convinced this girl was a kook at best, a dangerous con artist at worst.

Liza woke briefly that evening and insisted that Agent 28 outside her room call her Mom, then had to correct herself and say Liza's mother, Mrs. Penny Lang, and explain to her that her daughter was safe and sound. Liza made him repeat what he was going to say to her in explicit detail. Then she coached him to say to her mom that, her daughter, "Was a hero of whom she could be especially proud. She wouldn't be coming home for another day or so, and that the Paragon himself would be bringing her home. The Paragon body didn't have super hearing, but Liza was certain she heard her mother faint.

The next morning, Liza woke early and felt surprisingly well. No dizziness or aches or pains; in fact, she'd never felt better in her life. She thought about jumping out of bed and going out for a jog, a feeling she'd *never ever* had before. Dr. Suresh checked on her a few more times, and the psychiatrist ran his promised battery of tests that morning. He found the results odd, but there was nothing harmful or concerning, and so he ruled the Paragon fit to return to work. By early afternoon, so did Dr. Suresh after muttering how he was going to write a paper on the recuperative powers of the Paragon body.

Agent 28 had a wispy mustache and very blonde eyebrows, features Liza tried to memorize. It didn't help. She discovered 28 had the personality of a bar of soap and that he was easily forgettable. For example, when 28 brought her the Paragon's clothes, or as 28 called it, "The Uniform," he immediately returned to his post after uttering only the bare bone basics of human pleasantries.

Liza took a quick shower before getting dressed and was careful not to look and to touch as little as possible. When she had to touch, she did so only with a washcloth, and when she got out she hung a towel over the bathroom mirror. She was still having trouble getting the large body to move correctly, and she had banged the wall a few times. She also couldn't get her pants on while standing up. She tried to do it by sitting on the toilet and almost fell over, so she gave up and carried the pants out to the hospital bed. She lay down on the bed and shimmied the jeans up with a lot of wriggling. Just as Liza was pulling up the zipper, Cinaed walked in.

Liza recognized Cinaed immediately. Cinaed, pronounced kin-aye was one of the five team members who made up the Alpha Team commanded by the Paragon. She was in many ways as famous as the Paragon himself, but for different reasons. She was the party girl of the hero scene, and she always ended up in magazines in compromising and unflattering pictures, although she still managed to look good. Cinaed was Irish American, a natural ginger with impossibly long legs, and a way of walking that made people pay attention. Not that they could miss her while she was wearing her costume. A red spandex leotard with stylized yellow flames running up the sides, her suit was so tight there was nothing left for the imagination. She was a pyrokinetic, that meant that she could create fire and control it, but it was her reputation that tended to leave people with the most burns.

"About time you got up, John," she purred as she strutted right up to Liza and grabbed the Paragon's crotch. Liza's eyes went wide and she squeaked in shock.

"At least you're happy to see me." Cinaed grinned as she squeezed again.

"Are you out of your mind!" Liza yelled as she scooted back with enough force to send the hospital bed slamming into the far side of the room. Alarms from a dozen machines went off.

"Sorry, lover," Cinaed laughed. "I guess you're still mad." Cinaed did her best to look coy. "Would it help if I said I was sorry?"

Liza pulled on the Paragon's shirt. "Aren't you married?"

Cinaed laughed with an unattractive snort. "Since when did that matter, hon?"

"Are you serious?" Liza started putting the room back together.

"Well," Cinaed said leaning against the wall and crossing her arms, "what's got into you?"

Liza felt a headache forming between her eyes. "I just can't handle this right now. I mean you. I can't handle...I need you to leave."

"Are you serious?" The room warmed noticeably.

"Yes," said Liza trying to stop a machine from beeping and failing.

"*Fine. Be that way.*" Cinaed lit up. Her whole body was bathed in flame. A half second later the sprinklers and fire alarms went off, and she stomped out.

Liza stood there getting soaked as the agents and hospital staff began to evacuate the building. Then she noticed that only her hair was wet. "Huh. What do you know? His costume is waterproof."

A few hours later, Liza was sitting in an FBI conference room. The FBI agents complained a bit about having part of their office taken over, but when they saw the Paragon, they all wanted autographs for themselves and family members. Agents 22 and 23 were talking with the FBI and some local government folks. Liza wasn't sure what it was about, but from the snatches of conversations she overheard, she gathered it was about federal dollars for cleaning up after the incident in the mall. Agents 33 and 34 were on a conference call with headquarters that she was supposed to be a part of, but there were so many abbreviations and so much jargon that she had no idea what was being said, so she tuned out.

Cinaed showed up a little while later, saw Liza, and stayed out in the hall. Through the glass walls of the conference room, Liza watched Cinaed shamelessly flirt with every male she could find and was appalled to see every one of them fall under her spell.

Liza paid attention again when 34 said, "All charges have been dropped against Ms. Dunkirk, and she's been released from custody. We've had an FBI detail watch her, and we've tapped her phone line, but there's been no suspicious activity or communication. We've gotten back the full background check on her friends and family, and nothing of interest turned up that wasn't already in the preliminary report. She seems clean." To Liza's ears, he still sounded suspicious, and Liza wondered if she imagined it. Then she wondered if her unease around 34 was because he was black. She didn't seem to mind 33, but 34 made her uncomfortable in a way she couldn't articulate. She'd only known a handful of African-Americans in her life, and none of them well. When she was growing up, it had been common for her to witness varying levels of racism, but she always thought she free of it, but now she wasn't so sure. Logically he seemed like a nice guy - a family man, careful, cautious - but in her gut, when 34 was in the room, it made her nervous.

33 chimed into the call and explained that Colonel West had requested that she accompany him for a day, after which the Colonel would bring her home. That led to an hour's worth of security questions about what could be said around her, where she could be permitted to go, and how to amend the Colonel's itinerary. Apparently, the Paragon was supposed to be back in New York for some kind of staff meeting that was on hold until he returned.

34 concluded with, "I think that covers it, Colonel. Ms. Dunkirk is staying at the Holiday Inn under our nickel. You want us to pick her up, or do you want to fly?"

"Fly?" asked Liza, her face going pale. "I'm not feeling up for flying just yet."

"Pick up it is," said 33. "We've got wheels up to LaGuardia in two hours. I'll arrange to have her meet us at the jet."

34 gave Liza a sudden thumbs-up. "Sir? I'll make the flight smooth as silk."

"You're the pilot?"

"I know you hate planes, Colonel, but you haven't flown with me."

33 added, "He used to be a fighter pilot. I'll make sure he doesn't show off."

"Uh…thanks. I appreciate it." Liza swallowed hard. She'd never been on a plane before, so she was glad the Paragon didn't like them; her anxiety wouldn't be acting. "Is Cinaed going with us? We had a little fight this morning."

"Little?" Laughed 33. "She flew in on Defense Force 2 and asked to go back out as soon as they refueled."

"Yeah, little. Hospital's suing us for water damage," muttered 34. "And the bill for use of their facilities was already pure extortion."

Liza noticed the sleepy looks in both of their eyes and wondered if they'd slept. "Thanks for all of your hard work. Both of you. And them, too." Liza gestured to Agents 22 and 23 on the other side of the glass.

Both looked shocked, and there was an awkward silence. Eventually 34 said, "Thank you, Colonel. That means a lot, coming from you."

"Then I'll remember to say it more often."

They rode in a Hummer to the airport. It was huge inside and customized with enough comforts they may as well have taken a limo. When they hit traffic, they turned on flashing red and blue lights and drove around it on the berm. 33 used the lights again to run a stop light and later to make an illegal turn. They flashed badges and went right past the security checkpoint. The agents and Liza rode a little golf-cart-like car out to a sleek black jet that looked like it only seated about 12 people. The stairs leading into the plane made squeaking noises when Liza walked up. She had to duck her head to get in. Inside it was filled with big cushioned seats, each with a video monitor mounted above. The whole plane tilted noticeably where she walked, and Agents 33 and 22 sat on the opposite side of the plane in the front, while she was in the back and 34 went into the cockpit. Liza began to wonder how much the Paragon weighed, recalling that even the Hummer moved with the weight of his body.

Not long after she sat down, and 22 had served her a coke that she declined adding rum to. 23 arrived, and escorted John onto the plane. She watched John walk down the aisle in her body and decided he was having as hard a time adjusting as she was. John sat across the aisle from her, as there was only one row of seats on either side.

There was silence between them for awhile as the plane warmed up. By the time they were taxiing down the runway, both had death grips on the arms of their chairs, and Liza kept letting go when she heard or felt the chair arm crack or bend, only to absently do it again. The acceleration and surge up into the air made Liza close her eyes until they snapped open when she felt the thud of the landing gear being retracted. Having never flown, she was unaccustomed to the sensation of wheels being retracted, she looked out the window in panic. She thought a piece of the plane had fallen off or broken. The view out the window was stunning as Columbus shrank in the distance and waves of green trees and orange fields and tiny slivers of roads filled her view. She couldn't look away for a long time as she tried to recognize things from the air. She loved how houses looked like toys and cars like ants. Then the plane was hit with a pocket of turbulence that shook the little jet hard before they climbed above it.

"How do you normals stand it?" grumbled John. "At least, before, I could fly if the plane went down."

"You can fly again. Just get me the hell out of this body," said Liza, eyes closed, teeth grinding.

"We've been over this. You find Dr. Psi, and then we'll figure it out. Until then, you're me."

"I don't want to be you. You're an arrogant jerk who sleeps with married women."

"Oh, I see you met my Kinny."

"You could have warned me, John."

"No warning covers Cinaed. And she's not really married."

"I watched it on TV. She has a ring."

"Her hubby, CyberSoldier, is a limp wristed poseur." John made a downward waving gesture with his left hand.

Liza opened her eyes and gave John a sideways look. "What are you talking about?"

John sighed and leaned back in his chair and scratched his inner thighs in an impolite manner. "How do you put up with the itching from shaving? It's driving me crazy."

"You get used to it. And you're evading."

"Fine. I'll spell it out for you. CyberSoldier is gay. He bumps uglies with other boys. He's also still military and wants his pension. Since they passed "Don't Ask Don't Tell," he covers up his sex life. Cinaed is his beard."

Liza gave him a blank look.

"You really don't get out much, do you? Cinaed is his cover. It's a marriage of convenience. Nothing more."

"So Cinaed secretly sleeps with you?"

"Yes, genius, only it's not so secret. She cultivates a reputation that she sleeps with everyone, married or not. He thinks it's better to have a wife who runs around than to let on that he cups balls for fun." John looked out the tiny window. "Truth is, she can't sleep with anyone. Her slutty act is all a ruse. When she's aroused, she can't control her powers worth a damn. Burns the bed and anyone in it with her. I'm one of the few people in the world she can have sex with and not kill in the process."

"Oh, that's horrible!"

John scowled. "Hey, I'm not that bad."

"No. I meant that it's horrible she can't…"

"Can't say it, huh? You're something else. And I got it. I was just messing with you. And I agree. It's pretty awful. I can't stand her, but I give her a pity screw on occasion because it's the right thing to do."

"I can't decide if that's nice of you or awful. Awful is winning."

"I can't decide, either, so mostly I avoid her."

"What other dark secrets do I need to know?"

John looked at Liza. "It's only a two-hour flight."

"Someone is going to figure this out. The agents already know something's funny."

"Eh, don't worry. They change agents all the time. They all think we're crazy, and they all look the same to me. I gave up on their numbers a long time ago since they keep giving out the numbers to new guys. I just say, 'Hey you.'"

"That's not very nice."

"Do you know your mailman's name, or your local fireman?"

"As a matter of fact, I do. William. And the fire chief's name is Jack. I know everybody's name."

"Well that might be fine for your one-horse town, but there's a whole world out there. Six billion people. Every one of them knows my name, but I'll be damned if I learn theirs."

"They don't know your name. They know the Paragon's name. Who was John West before he was the Paragon?"

"A nobody."

"How did you become the Paragon?"

"None of your business."

"It is my business. It may come up."

"It won't come up."

"Are you sure?"

"Of course I'm sure."

"Well," said Liza thinking for the moment, "it might give us a clue as to how we can change back."

"You don't gain the powers by switching brains. The powers move on. You try that, and you'll still be stuck in my body, but with no powers."

"How do the powers change bodies?"

"None of your business."

"You're impossible."

"You're fat."

"What?"

"You heard me. I couldn't believe all the stretch marks when I looked in the mirror. You let this body go to waste."

"I did no such thing. I have a glandular problem."

"When was the last time you went to the gym or ate a carrot?"

"Not all of us are born with the bodies of Greek gods."

"You think I was? Hell no. The powers don't care what your body shape is. But I have a reputation to uphold. I need to look the part. Three hour workouts, daily. I'll bet you already put ten pounds on me."

"I've been in a hospital bed that *you* put me in."

"Eat a carrot."

"You're an asshole."

John laughed. "You don't know the half of it."

5

For the remainder of the flight, they didn't speak to each other. John slept like he didn't have a care in the world, while Liza stared blankly out the window, her face sullen and her arms crossed. She'd never been in a plane before, but, despite looking out the window, she couldn't focus on the experience and didn't register the view. She was so frustrated that it took all of her will not to cry, scream or punch John into next Thursday, but she managed to keep it all in. She kept telling herself she'd endured worse, that she could handle this, and eventually she did.

The landing was perfect, as gentle as a hummingbird. Liza was expecting worse as she saw the ground coming up, and when the bump came from the wheels dropping down and the tiny jet roared with noise, she instinctively braced for impact. She braced herself so hard, her super strength bent the aluminum frame of her chair arm and dented the floor plate.

A limo was parked and waiting on the tarmac where the plane taxied, and Liza, since she never flew, thought nothing of how odd it was. Riding in a limousine was another new experience, and she drank in the smell of old leather as the doors opened. As she sat, she was surprised to see the agents sit on seats that faced the wrong way, their backs to the driver and their faces to her. They sat John between them, and John stared at the mini bar as the car pulled away, but he didn't ask for anything to drink.

Liza wanted to watch as the Big Apple rolled past, but the windows were darkly tinted and their route took them into tunnels most people were unaware existed. She didn't get to see the skyscrapers and really had no sense of the city whatsoever. She drummed her fingers nervously on her thigh and wished for the ride to be over. The trip ended after what felt like hours to Liza, but it was only fifteen minutes. She had no clue that the trip would have been impossible if they'd taken public roads.

They got out in an underground parking garage. The garage was immaculate and contained only black vehicles of various types, all of them large.

"Welcome to headquarters," John whispered.

A cavernous, well-lit elevator carried them upwards at a good clip, but it still took ten minutes to arrive at their floor. On arrival, the elevator stopped so abruptly that Liza's stomach flip-flopped.

The doors opened into a vast office complex filled with cubicle dividers and desks of glass and steel. The cube pattern was interrupted occasionally by massive support columns, but otherwise the view was wide open all the way to the windowed walls. Video monitors were scattered about like fireflies in a field, and bustling workers leaped about like crickets answering phones, flitting about, and typing on huge beige computers. Some were identifiable as agents because of their black suits and earpieces, others were simply well dressed in business clothes. Every racial type Liza could think of was represented here, and she picked up the chatter of a dozen languages, or what she guessed were other languages, but she didn't know for sure.

The building was round so any direction Liza turned, that didn't face the elevators, looked out over the city. Hidden among the cubicles, which she didn't see at first, were conference rooms encased in glass. In each one she could see a variety of heated discussions going on. Wherever she looked, the floor was humming with urgent activity and a sense of accomplishment seemed to be hang in the air like old lady perfume.

The agents nodded to her as they moved past Liza to be swallowed up by the organized chaos. Liza was left staring openmouthed in awe by the elevator door, while John, looking bored, stared at his nails.

"You're making a scene," said John. "Close your mouth and head over to that big round desk to your right, the one with the huge office chair. That one's mine - I mean yours."

"I have a desk? I thought you just did super things."

"Super things require paperwork. And not every moment is an emergency. Now go over there. I'll show you how to log in."

They walked over and sat down, and as they entered the semi-circular area, the room noise fell away. "Silence field," said John. "You can control it from this panel here. This way makes it louder with room noise, or this way to totally cancel it out." John turned the dial and the room went silent. It was like watching a movie on mute. "You and I can hear each other, but no one outside of this area can."

"This is amazing!"

"I suppose." John sat on the edge of his desk. His new legs didn't reach the floor so he idly kicked them back and forth as he talked. He told Liza how to log into his computer, and when she did it, he got down, pushed her out of the way, and checked his email and messages. It was her turn to be bored, so she spun about in his overstuffed black leather office chair.

After a time, Liza noticed all the file cabinets and drawers underneath the big semicircular desk. She rolled up to one and started flipping through it. John didn't seem to notice or object, so she kept poking around. All dull stuff. She figured out that most of them were case files on missions of which the Paragon had been a part. The files were all about natural disasters: hurricane clean up, floods, fires, earthquakes, that kind of thing. The occasional photo in the dossiers was interesting, but not much else was. She poked around and found a different cabinet that held files on powered villains and terrorists, but the files were thin with little actual information. Over his shoulder John said, "Most of the information is on the network drives. Those are just printouts or personal notes. The good stuff is in encrypted files."

"So when do we do the hero stuff?" Liza said as she closed the file drawer.

"Depends. Whenever an alert comes in. Until then, we sit around, or hang out in the lounge or gym, or get out of here and let the pager alert us."

"Pagers?"

"It's a communicator built into the neckline of the costume. A throat mic picks up subvocal sounds so you can think about talking and it will pick it up without you saying a word. It also has a parabolic speaker that projects into your ear with no spillover so only you can hear it. Very high-tech, but I'm old-school, I just call it a pager."

"How old are you?" Liza said, realizing the biographies never said.

"Sixty-three. My powers slow my aging. As it was explained to me, everybody's cell divide, over and over, copying their DNA each time. But the ends of that DNA?

They fray over time, and it's that fraying causes aging. Mine don't fray. Part of my super healing." John turned around and kicked Liza in the knee.

"*Ow!* Why did you do that?" Liza rubbed her shin.

"Give it a second."

"Huh. It doesn't hurt anymore."

"The nerves respond to pain like normal, but they shut down quickly since the body isn't really being hurt. I could kick you hard enough to break my foot, or rather your foot, and it would hurt like hell, but after a second you wouldn't feel it."

"You had to kick me to tell me that?"

"Imagine bullets. They hurt like a son of a bitch. Tear up your clothes. But a few seconds later? Nothing."

"Great. So I'm indestructible, but it still hurts?"

"Only for a bit. You need to learn to ignore the initial pain."

"How the hell am I going to do that?"

"Practice. I used to shoot my foot every morning with a forty-five to help me wake up. Works better than coffee."

"You're nuts."

"I dive into volcanoes and stop civil wars. You have to be nuts to do that."

"Civil wars? You're serious?"

"Sometimes. Ever since the UN Powers Disarmament Treaty, it's been illegal to use powered beings in warfare. Countries still do it all the time, just like they all have poison gas stockpiles and nuclear weapons. So if the UN Security Council gives the go ahead, we have the authority to go in and stop them, and stop them so well that the targets never think to do it again. It's our main job, to act as a super-powered deterrent, but we almost never have to. No country likes outside interference, so everyone plays behind-the-scenes politics to keep us out. So what we mostly do is handle natural disasters. That's easy to approve in the council, but you'd be surprised at the number of countries that refuse our help anyways. Occasionally we help Interpol or respond to government requests to deal with powered nut jobs."

He paused and then continued, "Even though few people have powers by percentage, there's a lot of people in the world. So statistically small or not, it's still a lot of people with dangerous abilities. And people are people. So there is always a percentage that will use their powers for stupid shit. Wife beaters, rapists, drunken brawlers, frat boys, only with more oomph behind their bullshit. It's rare to find a true psycho like Dr. Psi, or super-powered crooks that rob banks and the like, but when it does happen it gets a lot of press because it's exciting. So people think it's more common than it is. You know how people fear dying in planes yet will drive cars despite the evidence that says cars are the real death trap? It's that kind of thing. Why rob a bank when people will give me fistfuls of cash for being me? Hollywood can, and has, offered to pay me to do stunts no normal could do. Crime is stupid. But like I said, there's a lot of people in the world. There will always be a few fanatics who believe this or that and who are willing to use their powers to punish everyone who thinks differently. That drawer you were looking at has a lot of those. Those are the *real* problem types."

"I had no idea."

"Of course not. Some stuff we kill before it gets reported. The agents are good at that. The reporters who don't play ball though...Control takes care of them."

"What's Control? I heard that term before. In the hospital I think."

"Not a what, a who. Control is the geekiest guy you'll ever meet, and he has the best nerd gear in the world. He's kinda the switchboard operator for all the agents and field heroes. You know that 1984 book? He's kinda like Orwell's bigger brother, and we got 'em. I don't think he sleeps. He's always on a computer. He calls it online. Here, I'll show you."

John double tapped the back of the forearm on the Paragon costume, and suddenly Liza's ears were filled with discussions. A gravelly male voice cut in, "You've got to stop putting me on mute. I've been calling you for hours. We've got a situation," and then fell silent as John tapped it again.

"I saw your face," said John, "what happened?"

"Control is mad you've been offline. And there's a situation."

"There's always a situation, and Control is always mad at me. Whenever your mic is on, Control is always tapped in. Just ask for anything and he'll make it happen. Order pizza, send out your dry cleaning, divorce your wife, anything. He has a whole team of nerds working for him. They live for this crap. But the string attached? He's a pain in the ass. Everything is dire and urgent with him, so I mostly shut him off unless I'm on a mission. If he *really* needs me, he sends an agent."

Liza's eyes were saucer wide. "There's no way I can do all this."

"Until we find Dr. Psi, you have no choice. You have to."

"Why do we have to find him? Why can't we tell Control and get this room full of men in black to do it? Let *them* find him."

"Because they don't really work for you. Sure, it's Colonel this and Colonel that, but they really work for UNSD, and so do you. If they find out you are not me, the first thing they'll do is bench you. Then it will be like I told you. Doctors will crawl out of the woodwork like roaches and they'll poke and prod you to figure out how it happened. Then they'll lock you away as a security risk until they decide what to do with you. They can't afford to have an uncontrolled and untrained power at my level just wandering around loose in the world. And while they screw around debating what to do with you, every whack job and terrorist will find out we don't have *me* around to deter them, and it will be like giving kids sugar. The deaths that would result will be on your hands."

"You're serious?"

"Of course I'm serious, you ditz. I've lived through this before, back when I first became the Paragon. That dipshit Bill just decided to quit one day and picked a random guy and made him the Paragon. That guy was tending bar, just minding his own business, and doing what he could to get by, and then suddenly his life was flipped upside down. My parents were hauled off to witness protection. To this day, I don't even know where they are, or if they're even still around. But that's the good part, because they were too slow to get to my kid and my ex. They didn't make it."

"Oh my God."

"Cut their throats and filmed it. Indonesian separatists. You tell me how killing my little girl helps solve anything in a pissant little country half a world away? But that's how the world thinks. Crazy ass shits, the lot of them."

John was staring off into the distance and silence hung in the air between them.

Liza asked, gently, "How old was she?"

"Six. Emily...was six. Her mother hated my guts and left when she got pregnant and didn't even tell me about my kid at first. But sure enough, when her money ran out she came around for handouts and then vanished again until the next time she needed money. I barely ever saw Emily, and she didn't know who I was. It was a mess of the first order, but it was also forty years ago. Water under the bridge. Just believe me when I tell you to shut your mouth until we fix this."

Liza had no idea what to say, and John didn't seem to want to hear anything. He turned his back to her and began typing away at his computer. It was disorienting for Liza. The sympathy and sorrow she felt inside were different from John's cold and distant emotions coming out of her body. It was like watching herself in a mirror and seeing someone else respond.

John began searching through desk drawers until he found something small that he put into his ear. It was small enough to disappear into the ear canal. "Ok. I set up my backdoor channel. We had some private com channels put in for various reasons that I'm not getting into with you. What you're going to do now is turn on your suit's pager and say "John John" before you talk. That's a code word. Everything you say from that point on will only be heard by me. When you're done talking to me you say "Over." That will put you back on the normal com channel, which I will also be listening to. Regardless of the channel, anything I say to you will only be heard by you."

"I don't get it. John John?"

John frowned. "You just turned it on. Now you need to say 'Over'."

"Over?"

John looked up and touched his ear. "Yeah. That did it."

"This is ridiculous."

"Kinny set it up. She thinks it's funny. I hate it, and she knows it. But it's preset into the backdoor, and I don't know how to change it, so we'll use it. Ready to try?"

"I guess so."

"This is easy stuff. We'll practice for a bit while I'm next to you and work out the kinks. Then we'll be in touch, no matter how far apart we are physically."

"Planning on going somewhere without me?"

"Control said there was a situation. Second you go back online, he'll be hounding you. Pretty soon, you'll be off somewhere, and little girl me won't be allowed to go with you. That, and pretty soon I'll have to go back to corn town and pretend to be you."

The panic was clear in Liza's eyes. "I don't know how to fly! How can I be you if I can't fly?"

"That's you're biggest concern? You have weird priorities. Just think about jumping, but don't move your legs."

"Really? That's it?" Liza immediately shot up and bumped her head on the ceiling hard enough to push the sound insulation panel out of place as she hovered in the air.

John smirked. "Imagine the feeling in your legs when you land from a jump."

Liza landed on the ground with a thud. Sound dampeners made it a silent thud from the rest of the room, but several people felt it and looked around for the source.

"That's it." John said, barely suppressing laughter. "The rest is practice. Lots and lots of practice. If I were you, I'd fly around whenever you can until you get the hang of it. Until you get it, though, tell everyone it's a side effect from Dr. Psi's attack and that the doc said you should get better soon. That should be a good enough cover story."

The panic had not left Liza's eyes. If anything it was worse. John pointed at her arm and touched one hand to his ear. Liza blinked. Then she stared at her arm and eventually double tapped her forearm to activate the pager.

"Don't hang up on me again, Paragon! I need you in the war room now!"

John nodded to indicate he had heard and then crossed his arms. "You didn't turn on the private channel."

"John John. What's the war room and where is it?"

John whispered but sounded crystal clear in Liza's ear. "It's our briefing room two floors up. Head to the elevator and hit the star-shaped button with the line under it. When it opens, go to the end of the hall. Go in the door that says *War Room*. When you go in, make sure you say out loud who is in there because I can't see. I'll stay here to coach you, plus I have to clear up a few loose ends. Tell Control to send 33 to babysit me while you're gone or people will get suspicious."

Liza hesitated and then said in a whisper, "Control, I have a guest. A young woman. Can you have 33 watch her while I head up?"

John frowned. "You didn't say *Over*."

Liza said, "Over" and then repeated herself. Control complied, and soon 33 got up from his desk and was walking over to them.

"Thanks, Control," Liza added.

John frowned even more. "I never thank Control."

"You never thank anyone, as far as I can tell," Liza snapped.

"Uh, ok. Sorry, Colonel," said Control.

Liza's face turned bright red, "I didn't mean you, Control. I was talking to someone else. Sorry."

"I don't say sorry either," said John.

"John John. Bite me. Over."

"If you're going to sound like me, you need to act like me. Now get going," said John.

Liza bit back some choice responses and instead stalked off for the elevator. As she moved, she had the unpleasant feeling that the whole room was watching her. She pushed the up button and half expected alarms to go off identifying her as a fraud. "I'm out of my mind for doing this," she muttered.

"Come again, Colonel? I didn't make out that last part," said Control.

"You'll be fine," said John.

Liza tapped the suit mic off. She doubted anything would be fine ever again.

6

The elevator moved silently until it dinged on the floor marked with a star shape. Liza walked out into a corridor that had only one door at its end. As she walked on the black marbled floor, the Paragon's snake skin boots clacked like a hammer no matter how carefully she walked. The walls were covered in large panels of plain white metal or shiny plastic. She couldn't tell which without tapping, and she didn't want to try that. Each panel was adorned with a large framed photographs of the Defense Force members doing amazing things. Liza took her time looking at them, unwilling to reach the other end of the hall. She recognized most of the heroes in the pictures, though some took guesswork to identify because the faces looked so young. Comparing before and after, she decided that hero work must age people, like how presidents go gray in office. The Paragon being the exception to the rule, he looked the same. There were also a few faces scattered amongst the photos that she didn't recognize at all. It was easy to find Cinaed in several of them, her pyrokinetic abilities doing impossible things by shaping or moving fire. She always looked confident in every picture, as if she were playing to the cameras. The other heroes showed fear or anger on occasion, but Cinaed was always happy and cocky. The Paragon was always serious looking or flashing a fake smile. That struck her as odd, because she'd seen his picture countless times in magazines and never thought his smile looked fake before. The few times she'd seen John smile in her body, it had carried a tinge that was mocking or snide, and now she saw the same in John's pictures.

The war room entrance was a double door, each half emblazoned with a star made of opaque frosted glass. The remainder of the door had a mirrored finish, and Liza stared at the strong jawline of Paragon for a bit. She paused to make faces, trying to decide what looked strong on John instead of revealing the freaked out Liza underneath. She settled on a grimace that looked a bit like she was chewing nails, or possibly that she had a toothache, she couldn't decide which. She swallowed hard and decided it had to be chewing nails because she was the Paragon. She was the badass.

She reached for the door and it slid aside on its own.

Legends filled the room. It was not a large room. It had five sides and was just big enough for a large pentagonal conference table made of something smooth and black with a white star inlaid in the middle. A chair faced each point of the star, and there was a bit of space to walk around the table, but not much. The walls were lined with video monitors that left very little wall exposed. The legends were arranged around the table, but Shokkusan was the only person in her seat. Her arms were crossed, and she was scowling. It made her eyes look like thin black lines and drew down her plucked eyebrows into a fierce V. Her jumpsuit was blinding neon yellow with diagonal jagged black slashes dancing up each side. Her hair was short and spiked like each strand was trying to escape her head. Shokkusan was an electrokinetic; she controlled electricity the way Cinaed controlled fire. Liza knew she was asian, and thought she was of Japanese descent, but couldn't remember for sure if that was correct. To Shokkusan's right was the CyberSoldier standing with his arms crossed. He was an extremely tall man with deathly pale white skin that was mostly covered with articulated chrome plates of armor with cables snaking in and out. The armor was partially covered by army green fatigues with a million utility pockets and black steel-toed boots. His face was the only part not armored, though in the hall she'd seen most of his face covered. His nose looked like it had been broken a few times and a scar ran across his right eye, which split his eyebrow in the middle. He was loudly arguing about something with the Blurr, and spittle was flying from his mouth as he talked. The Blurr was hard to make out because he was a blue gray blur of movement that never was in one place. He seemed to be gesturing and talking with his hands, but nothing could be clearly distinguished. Liza knew that the Blurr looked a lot like the hot Latin guy from the movie Desperado. She tapped her chin until she could remember the actor's name: Antonio Banderas. But seeing the Blurr in person, she couldn't discern much of anything. On the other side of the boys, Cinaed leaned against the wall, bored, and filing her nails, occasionally looking at her efforts.

No one looked up as she entered, but a face took over one of the video screens. The face belonged to a young twenty-something boyish-looking man who was overdue by a day or so for a shave and who wore glasses too large for his face. His short hair needed washing, and he hid it under a black Babylon 5 baseball cap worn backwards. His black t-shirt was ratty enough to qualify as vintage. Something written on it in white that Liza couldn't make out because the camera cut it off. The image said, "Colonel. Welcome. We can begin the in brief."

All of the monitors sprang to life, and the Minnesota skyline scrolled across several of the wall screens with the Metrodome dominating the view. Surrounding the Metrodome was a sea of green and yellow figures moving and swaying like a field of grass. The star in the table went gray and changed into a video screen projecting an overhead view of the football stadium's white dome. Liza didn't understand what she was looking at, but she decided the figures looked to be at least twice the size of a human, and they had yellow triangular heads with green torsos on exaggeratedly stocky bodies.

"You have got to be kidding me," said the CyberSoldier as he slapped his hands on the table with a dull clanging sound.

The image replied, "Not kidding, Cyber. This is not a hoax. We're guessing a deranged fan took his rivalry too far. I'm estimating five thousand robots on all sides of the Metrodome. There was a Vikings game in progress, which means we have about sixty thousand plus hostages."

"I like robots," said Shokkusan, arcing electricity idly between her fingers and smiling mischievously.

"At the moment, they've taken up a defensive position and no one has made demands," said the image. Liza decided this had to be Control. He continued, "but the robots defended themselves forcefully when efforts were made to remove them. We have reports of a hundred injuries so far. A few are critical." Liza couldn't reconcile the professional adult voice coming out of the geeky man-child image on the screen. With the agents in black, and the military uniforms she saw scattered about, she wondered how Control got away with wearing what he wanted. She kinda liked that. One sort-of normal person in this wonderland of not-normal.

"There's going to be a lot more injuries than that soon," said Cyber. "Painted like that, it's just pouring gasoline on a campfire."

"Honey," Cinaed said, sounding bored, "less drama and more details."

Control answered for him, "The robots are dressed to resemble football players from the rival team, the Green Bay Packers. This stunt was clearly meant to provoke the Minnesotans."

Liza spoke up without realizing she was talking out loud. "So why do they have triangle heads if they're supposed to be football players?"

"Are you serious, Paragon?" yelled Cyber. "Look closely. Those are *cheese heads*!"

He said it in such a way that Liza felt she ought to know what that meant, so she did her best to play along. "*Oh!* You're right. Those bastards in their… cheesiness." Liza waved her arms about in outrage. CyberSoldier nodded in agreement, so Liza growled back and wondered if she should thump her chest. Based on her brother Davey's behavior, that seemed to be standard male communication when team loyalty was involved.

A squeal of high-pitched noise emanated from Blurr and Control said, "You're right, Blurr. This is a person who clearly wants attention. The playoff game was already widely covered, but now every news channel is involved."

The images on the walls changed to show the TV coverage from a dozen channels, but no sound. Control added, "I've been trying to hack into a robot's operating system by scanning for the wireless signals being used to manipulate them, but I haven't found an opening. The machines seem to have a limited amount of autonomy, but I believe they are commanded centrally. What I have been able to do is triangulate the Internet traffic surges to isolate the general locale of the servers he's using. I think I can knock him offline, but unless I can get a better fix, it will have to be a brute force attack that will take most of the Midwest offline. But we're not allowed to do that anymore. After the Cupertino mission, we're under new regulations to not disrupt an Internet backbone because of all the government and banking systems that now rely on them. There's also no telling what the robots are programmed to do when they become completely autonomous."

"Like Prague," said Cinaed.

"Exactly," said Control.

"Prague?" asked Liza.

"Where those copper men all exploded when we put that big mainframe down," said CyberSoldier. "I don't know where you were. I think dealing with neo-Nazi arsonists in Germany or something. That was only two years ago. Don't you ever read a report?"

"*Guys!*" yelled Shokkusan, "*Focus!*"

"We need an all-female team," said Cinaed.

"That would be too productive for government work," said Shokkusan.

"What do you think, Colonel?" asked Control, "How should we play this?"

All eyes turned to Liza. Liza put her arms behind her back and quickly tapped her suit and mumbled, "John John. Listen."

As soon as the mic was enabled John asked, "I saw the Cheeseheads on a newsfeed. That the mission?"

"Well," said Liza out loud to the room, repeating the situation for John's benefit, "If we cut the servers that support the cheese robots, there might be, um, back up servers? Or maybe there is a decentralized way to control them? That's why the only safe thing to do is cast a wide net and take down the entire Midwest's Internet. Right?

But doing that would have deep consequences. We can't just shut it off willy nilly."

Shokkusan blinked. "Did you just say willy nilly?"

Control added, "I think it's a risk within an acceptable window, Colonel."

"It's too easy a choice. I think it's misdirection for something else," said Liza, suddenly smiling, "like a mob pull." Liza's memory had jumped to playing miniatures in high school on Saturdays at the comic bookstore: metal figures of orcs and elves all painted up and wearing space marine armor and arranged to represent armies. The figures attacked each other based on dice roles, game rules, and player choices. It was a silly game and the guys that played it were rude to new players, so she mostly watched, but she'd picked up a few things. "It's like kiting. They're using a lure to draw us where they want us, making us do what they want. They're leading our reactions."

Everyone stared at Paragon, some open-mouthed.

"Possible," said Control. "This does look like a staged gimmick to be as attention-getting as possible. But why? An attack elsewhere? To trick us into dropping the network?"

"To what end?" asked the CyberSoldier in a whiny voice while sitting down and giving the Paragon a look that suggested ice water was now being served by Satan using flying pigs as waiters.

John added, "You do know you are the smash first, think later guy right?"

Liza shook her head. She had a nagging hunch in her gut that she just knew she was right about. If only she could piece it together into a tangible thought. "Control. Check the stock market." Liza drummed her fingers on the table. "I read about something like this. Last summer a backhoe snapped a main hub cable in Atlanta. The Net was down for the entire Eastern seaboard for a couple of minutes. When it came back up there were automatic stock sell and buy orders queued up from a hacker. They suspended all electronic trading, but it was already too late. The hacker had bought and sold thousands of shares for pennies on the dollar and made millions. The money was all routed offshore and the hacker was never caught."

Control finished the thought: "The Black Bear heist. But all the regulations changed after that. There are too many safeguards and redundancies in place now for that to happen. Everything's been hardened to prevent hackers from pulling a repeat. The only way a hub can go down completely at this point is if the government does it with an emergency order…and that's what I was going to do…" Control, thinking out loud, tapped a pen on his lips. "The U.S. markets are closed on Sunday…but overseas trading doesn't stop. Let me do some digging." His image went away.

"Hello?" yelled CyberSoldier. "Giant robots here! We need to take these things out, not play Star Wars!"

Liza had had enough of him. "Do you really think a football fan built those robots to disrupt a game?"

"It's not a game, it's the playoffs!" Cyber argued.

Liza gestured with her hands to pantomime that he was crazy. "A prank with one or two I could see, but hundreds? And to hold a stadium hostage? Without taunting? Without making demands? Nope. This is a diversion."

"I hate to say it," said Shokkusan, "but Para-Ego is right."

"Para-Ego?" asked Liza.

"You prefer Para-cojones?"

"That's Spanish for balls," added John in an amused voice.

"I know what it means!" Liza yelled, and everyone gave her a strange look. "Well I do, and I don't like it. My name is Paragon. Use it."

"I'm back," said Control. "You may be onto something, Colonel. The NSA has been tracking unusual activity from a syndicate in Eastern Europe. Global stocks are jittery in Shanghai right now, so a sell off could create a tailspin. We're looking into it, but I think the risk is real. So what's the plan?"

Before she could open her mouth, John shouted in Liza's ear, "Hit the robots and keep the attention on the Metrodome. Then let nerd boy figure out how to block the computer stuff."

"We split into two teams," said Liza. "Most of us will take on the robots."

"*Sweet!* Now we're talking!" said Shokkusan.

"Meanwhile," Liza continued, "Control can narrow down where the commands are coming from and Blurr will then manually cut those connections to the outside world. That way we don't have to take down the whole Internet; we'll just disconnect him."

Blurr made a noise, and Control said, "Might work. Lots of variables, though. Blurr, I'll talk you through what to do and what to look for while you're crossing country. I'll get the Hawks prepped for the rest of the team."

"That's the black jets you flew in today," said John. "With proper clearance we can take them to supersonic speeds. Lucky you, you get to fly again. Let Cinaed and Shoku hit the robots and Cy-lady can shoot at them. You take crowd control and protect the dome. Odds are nothing out there can harm you, so it should be easy. Anything gets in your way? Punch it."

Liza tried to make her voice sound macho. "I'll protect the dome and the civilians. The rest of you get to make a mess. Tear 'em up."

Shokkusan looked up in surprise. "You're taking a back seat? You know there are cameras out there? Press?"

Cinaed raised an eyebrow and studied Paragon for a moment. "He's still recovering from the Dr. Psi mess. He's playing it safe. Nothing wrong with that."

CyberSoldier stalked out of the room. "Wheels up in five."

"Shotgun," called Shokkusan, as she followed him out. The Blurr had already left, unnoticed.

Cinaed got up from the chair slowly. "Screens off." The monitors turned off. "Privacy mode. Command code: *Bite me.*" The hum of background noise from the video screens faded. The room became as silent as a grave.

"I don't know what's going on with you," said Cinaed, "but I have your back." She crossed over to Paragon and kissed his cheek, "and I expect a *quid pro quo.* That's Latin. Look it up." Cinaed winked and left the room.

When Liza was by herself, she leaned on the table and hyperventilated a little. Then she straightened up and took several deep-cleansing breaths. Gwenifer had taught her to how to do that during one of her on-again/off-again fascinations with Yoga. It made her miss her friend terribly.

When she was ready, she asked, "John John. Does this pager thing work? John? How do I get to the plane?"

* * *

Liza joined the team in a comfortably equipped black minibus that sped away along another set of tunnels that Liza began to understand were not public. They emerged at an airfield on what Liza guessed was a military base. She had never seen a military base outside of the movies, but the huge gun emplacements stationed about, covered by camouflage netting, was a giveaway, along with the personnel in fatigues.

They drove right out onto the tarmac and up to the plane. They were met by agents who were prepping a second plane to follow them. CyberSoldier boarded the jet first and set himself down in the pilot's chair. Shokkusan sat next to him, which made Liza nervous. Random sparks would occasionally jump between Shokkusan and metal surfaces, and she made the hair stand up on Liza's Paragon arm when she was close by. Liza didn't think a cockpit full of electronics was the best place for her to be.

Within minutes, they were done with the pre-flight checks and were barreling down the runway and into the air. The acceleration was far more severe than what Liza had endured coming to New York, but she did her best not to damage the seat when she gripped it.

The plane banked hard when it turned, which twisted the cabin almost sideways, thus making Liza dent the aluminum hand rest of her chair. They climbed very quickly at an angle best reserved for roller coasters. The other members of the team didn't seem to mind, nor were they alarmed by Paragon's obvious panic.

Video monitors were installed in various places of the Defense Force plane allowing Control to continually update them on the situation. Shokkusan and Cyber were chatting in the cockpit, but Liza couldn't make out what was being said. Cinaed, seated midway in the back of the plane in a row of seats all by herself, was reading a novel. Liza caught a glimpse of a cover that was explicit enough that Liza was sure she was reading smut.

"What's wrong with these people?" thought Liza.

John answered, "What's wrong? A lot. What specifically are you asking about?"

"How did you hear that? I didn't say anything," Liza whispered.

"Subvocal. I told you. When you think about speaking your throat muscles move and this picks it up. You have to be careful how you think. You also need to remember to close the channel."

"Over!" She snapped, then looked around to see if anyone noticed. No one had.

There was one agent on the plane acting as a steward, and he had the third chair in the cockpit. Liza didn't recognize him and found she missed 33 and 34. They were people with families to her, and she wondered if she'd see them again.

The team and the agent ignored her for the entire flight.

John didn't ignore her. She'd turned the mic back on and he kept chattering randomly in her ear about how the team worked and didn't work. He flitted from topic to topic like a bee in a rose garden. Liza didn't pay attention to half of what he said, but the gist of it all sunk in.

The first concern was the very real danger from friendly fire. Cinaed, Shokkusan, and CyberSoldier were good at creating collateral damage according to John. The second point John made was that while only the Paragon could fly, CyberSoldier had enhanced strength and was fairly indestructible. Cinaed's and Shokkusan's powers did not have a long range, though Cinaed could affect any heat source and Shokkusan could change current back and forth between alternating and direct which tended to mess up electronic devices badly. Blurr always did his own thing, and only Control could reliably communicate with him. Most of the team tended to do their own thing, but they also tended to listen to Paragon, which annoyed CyberSoldier to no end. He always felt that he should be in charge. John had never actually been in the military; his rank of Colonel was honorary, mainly because the first Paragon was a Colonel and habits die hard. CyberSoldier, on the other hand, was originally a Marine Corps Major who lost all four limbs when a firefight broke out in a peacekeeping mission. He was protecting his own men at the time and was awarded a Purple Heart. When he went back stateside, testing determined he qualified genetically to be in a top secret program designed to make the 21st century warfighter. To date, he was the only one to survive the procedure. After his enhancements, he was deployed in every armed conflict in which NATO or the US participated, but officially he had no rank and was so covert he held no ID or status. For a long time he was even legally dead and didn't exist until he was assigned to the team and given the call sign CyberSoldier. From day one, Cyber felt that he should be leading the team and argued with John every chance he could. However, as John stressed, he was a good soldier and would always follow orders when it came right down to it.

Once John started in on Cyber stories, he didn't stop, and he got into some personal areas that Liza didn't want to know about. John told her that Cyber would always act over-the-top macho when he could, as if he had something to prove, and that he hit on Cinaed aggressively and proposed to her on their second date. They did a justice-of-the-peace wedding in Vegas two months later. It was Cinaed's idea. Cyber had tried to break up with her by the third date, but Cinaed had figured out why since she also fake-dated for appearances. Cinaed suggested they could help each other out with an 'open' marriage. The marriage was so open that they never shared a bed. John made a bunch of other hints that Liza didn't understand because she didn't want to, but it was clear that John disliked Cyber as much as Cyber disrespected John.

Liza was glad when the plane landed and John stopped gossiping. Apache helicopters were ready to go when they arrived. Paragon, as the only one who could fly, and because neither bullets nor missiles couldn't harm him, was supposed to fly escort while the rest of the team rode in the copter. Everyone else went straight from jet to copter without missing a beat while Liza shuffled her feet on the tarmac and looked up hopelessly for answers in the lightly clouded early evening sky. "I don't know how to *do* this. Think jump, but don't jump he said." She hopped about. "*How?*"

John was still listening, "You play those video games, right? Shoku always plays that plumber thing with the mushrooms. There's a jump button, isn't there? You don't jump in real life when you push the button, do you? Imagine you're jumping when the button is pushed."

"You're kidding right? I'm freaking out enough as it is and I really don't need teasing right now."

"Did you try it?"

"I was waiting for the helicopter to lift off."

"They're waiting for you. Jump."

Liza hopped in place a few more times, first one leg and then the other. She tried wriggling her butt like a cat ready to pounce and then tried to leap and stumbled forward. "It's not working. Nothing's working!"

She threw her hands up into the air in frustration and suddenly leapt a hundred feet into the air before she started falling. She spun her arms like a windmill and flailed about until she smacked into the ground face first.

"What the hell are you doing?" Cinaed asked over the suit com.

"How do I switch my channels again?" Liza thought. "Oh yeah."

"Over. I'm still woozy from yesterday, Cinaed. Give me a minute." Liza turned the suit mic off and cussed as she got to her feet and dusted herself off. She winced at the pain in her knees and the palms of her hands. She checked but of course they weren't scraped up no matter how much they felt like they were.

"I want to fly, but I can't even swim," she muttered to herself. "This is insane." She hopped a few more times and suddenly made a thirty-foot leap and landed awkwardly but didn't wipe out. "Damn it. I can't hop there. I can see the papers now. Paragon, the Super Frog."

She rocked back and forth on her knees and heels in a sprinting position and then ran forward with an explosion of speed. She couldn't comprehend how fast she was moving. She was a heartbeat from running out of runway. Liza closed her eyes and imagined she was a plane hurtling into the air as she made one last leap. There was a rush of wind, and she squinted to see that she had been propelled into the air by a super powered leap, but she wasn't flying. A feeling of weightlessness came over her as she reached the top of the mile-long arch, and she looked down to see a scrubby forest below her that she was going to fall onto. She squeezed her eyes closed and imagined bouncing on her bed as a child. Her mom had yelled at her and spanked her for doing it, but she did it anyway because it was fun, and it felt like flying sometimes.

At first she felt nothing other than the sensation of falling. She kept moving her shoulders up and imagined bouncing higher and higher when she suddenly felt as if she were lifting. It was like how she imagined a kitten felt being yanked up by the scruff of its neck by its mother. The falling slowed, but she was still falling. She concentrated harder, focusing on the image of being lifted by her neck, and the clearer she could picture the feeling, the slower her decent became, until she stopped falling altogether and was hanging in the air like a coat on a hanger. She imagined the hanger moving, and she moved through the air. She looked like a marionette being swung about by a drunk puppeteer, but she was flying.

She opened her eyes fully and nearly vomited. Each yank she gave herself made the world slide away and gave her instant vertigo. The helicopter roared past, and the copter going one way while she was going another was too much for her head to process. She lost it and threw up, but she somehow yanked herself in the opposite direction so she didn't hurl on herself.

The taste in her mouth was horrible, and when she thought about that and then by habit wiped her mouth, she lost her focus on flying and began to fall.

She tried next to yank herself up gently and failed. She tried again and jerked herself up. She tried again and again and slowly figured out how to pull herself up lightly enough that she was more or less floating. The floating was slow and gentle enough that the vertigo subsided. She opened her eyes and found the view beautiful, so beautiful that she was looking all around in wonder as the second copter turned back and hovered in beside her. Cyber had the door open and was leaning out and pantomiming tapping his forearm. Liza watched the copter hover around her and found she didn't mind if it was moving as long as she wasn't also moving.

She took the hint and turned on the com.

"Can you do this? Do we need to fly you?" shouted CyberSoldier. Liza wasn't sure if he was yelling because he was mad or because the helicopter was loud.

"I'm good. I got this," said Liza and she tugged herself up and the vertigo hit her like a wave. She closed her eyes, mentally yanked herself in the direction she was supposed to go, and took off like a rocket. The helicopter tilted and roared to catch up. "Control?"

"Yeah, Colonel?"

"I'm having trouble seeing. It's my eyes, Control. I've got something in them and they keep watering up. Can you guide me in?"

"Uh, ok. That's new. Sure. Head to your left twenty degrees. You overdid it. Right a little. There. Dead on."

"Thanks, hon. I don't know what I'd do without you."

"Hon?" said CyberSoldier. "What are you two? Queer?"

"Seriously? He calls *me* queer?" said John on his private line. "That guy needs to burst out of his closet and quit pretending it's bolted shut."

"Sorry, Control. That was meant for someone else. Forgot to turn the private channel on."

"Meant for whom?" said Cinaed over the com.

"Never mind! We've got a mission here! Let's just stick to it, shall we?" shouted Liza, hoping she sounded tough while hurtling in the general direction she wanted to go like a wobbly rocket missing a fin and with her eyes closed tight.

7

Flying blind got progressively easier. Liza was able to focus on what flying felt like, and it reminded her of flying in her dreams, dreams she'd mostly forgotten after waking, but of which she was perfectly aware when she was sleeping. Every turn she made thrilled her like carnival rides had when she was little. A memory found its way to the surface of her mind of a long ago lost uncle or cousin or someone swinging her through the air when she was a little girl. She had no idea who it was, but she remembered the feeling: the faith that she wouldn't fall, and the thought that she never wanted it to end.

Liza chanced to open her eyes and saw the city sprawling out beneath her, like the flipping pages of a picture book and the cars within it tearing off in all directions of the street grid like ants in a hurry to find a new home. It was too much to take in.

She closed them again, after she started spiraling wildly, and her heart pounded madly. Eyes closed, she was able to calm her trajectory and discovered she was holding her breath, so she forced herself to take slow steady breaths.

As Control guided her, Liza found she liked his voice. It was calm and friendly, not at all pretentious, though a little high pitched and squeaky when she flew the wrong way, though never enough to sound afraid. He was cool under pressure. He simultaneously kept the team up to date on the evolving situation, never missing a beat in his directions to her. She wondered if he had help, but, if he did, it was only his voice that kept them together, and with her eyes closed, it was like listening to the news on the radio. Dire problems around the world were summed up with reassurance, only the problems weren't around the world, they were right in front of her.

Control explained that the robots had begun marching in a series of concentric circles around the Metrodome. A few had casually shot up some police cars using high caliber munitions mounted on their arms and shoulders. Reports inside the dome concluded that people were beginning to panic and there was real danger of either a stampede or a riot. Beyond the ring of robots was a small army of police, SWAT, and National Guard, all tense and ready to fire. Buzzing about them was a flock of reporters dashing about.

Control chimed in that Blurr had reached the server farm. The plan now was for the team to engage the robots as a distraction before Control directed Blurr to pull the connections, or something like that. Liza wasn't sure. She was catching glimpses of the big white dome and, around it, the sea of green towards which she was hurtling. She tried hard not to think about the chaos she was approaching and focused on Control's soothing voice instead.

Control had changed to a private channel to guide her, sparing her more ridicule from the team, but that meant that he could shout now, which was unnerving. "Paragon! A news copter just flew in too close to the Cheese Bots.

They shot it down! It's falling onto the dome! You need to be there now!" She blinked. The absurdity of this entire mess hit her all at once. Then the panicked realization that real people were getting hurt sunk in. The responsibility of it all was overwhelming. It paralyzed her thoughts. By instinct alone, she was flying in the right direction, watching the vehicle spiral to its doom. She could tell that she wouldn't reach it in time, but had no idea what to do.

"You can go a hell of a lot faster, Liza," said John in her ear. "That dome isn't solid. It's fabric, and it's held up by fans. From what I'm seeing on the news, that bird is gonna bash right through it if you don't get your butt over there and catch it."

Liza shook herself, and tried to focus. She squinted and saw the burning wreck and imagined a rubber band tied to her shoulders that was stretching longer and longer until it snapped, and she shot forward like a rocket. The air screeched by her ears in a deafening roar. Her teeth clenched, and she squinted. The helicopter inflated like a balloon as she approached. It was spiraling in the air, not directly falling. The main blades were still spinning, keeping it slightly aloft, but the tail was gone, and the copter whipped about like a snake with its head cut off. Liza willed herself to go faster and aimed for the landing struts, certain she'd miss the wild thrashing thing.

"Hope I can stop," she thought in the heartbeat between flying and being jerked back in the opposite direction in a whip-snapping dead stop. "How did I do that?" she wondered as the copter slammed down onto her. It shoved her down with it and was spinning her about, thereby creating an all new overwhelming vertigo. She closed her eyes and willed herself up. The machine was lifted like a toy, and they spiraled up together into the sky, leaving only a few pieces of fiery debris to rain down onto the dome.

Keeping the vehicle aloft turned out to be the easy part. It was a lot harder to stop them from spinning than it was to simply stop flying forward, but in fits and starts, Liza figured it out. She heard distant cheers followed by a loud crack, and a missile shot arced past her hips, missing her by only a foot. Several more pops could be heard beneath the copter's roaring followed by a chorus of pops that sounded like bubble wrap being crumpled up. Accompanying the pops was the sudden prickle of a dozen dentist needles being jabbed into every part of her body. The pain was intense, but she kept enough of her wits about her to will herself higher into the air. The number of sharp jabs gradually decreased until there were none. Every spot stung and itched, but she couldn't touch them without dropping the helicopter, so she ground her teeth and felt her clenched grip dig into the metal as if it were soft mud.

Liza shuddered and took deep breaths before looking down to see the tiny white disk of the dome coated in the black flecks of her team's arriving copters. Arcs of flame were shooting out of the lead one, and flashes of lighting arced out of the next.

"We'll cover you and draw their fire," said Cinaed in her ear. "You find a place to put that thing down and get inside that dome."

After a frantic bit of guidance from both Control and John at the same time, Liza managed to set the helicopter down on a skyscraper roof. Her knees were shaking as she stood on solid ground, and she hugged herself and took a deep breath before checking and finding the passengers shaken but okay. With a gulp she ran off the edge of the building, leaped into the air, and flew off back to the Metrodome.

By the time she got there, the battle was in full swing. Arcs of lightning leapt about off of the metal behemoths while CyberSoldier matched their gunfire with even more gunfire. He'd mounted machine gun turrets to his arms and carried two more in his hands. Long chains of bullets rained out in all directions. Control had wisely directed the authorities to get back just as Cinaed shouted over the com, "You know what, you bastards? Nobody ever thinks to make an engine that'll survive overheating." The air rippled as heat waves rolled out and made the robots look like bobble headed toys as they staggered back from her.

"Confirmation. The robots are entering the Dome!" shouted Control, as Liza swooped down towards one of the main entrances. She drove down faster and faster and put her arms over her face as she smashed into a pile of robots that were squeezing through the gate. They shattered around her like a Lego building kicked apart by a child, but it felt as if she were being beaten in the face by the bats from an entire baseball team.

"Blurr's yanking the servers offline. Expect trouble," said Control, as Liza dug herself out of a pile of sparking and wiggling rubble. She stood up, a little shakily, and was surprised to hear applause. People who were cowering moments before were on their feet and cheering. At the first sign of trouble, the security gates had been lowered, but the robots had bent the bars apart enough to squeeze in and more were now trying to do the same. Liza shook her shoulders back and stretched out a kink, then lowered her shoulder and charged like a linebacker at the breech. She smacked into the machines with a *Kerrang*, and they were knocked back like dominoes. She grunted as she gripped the bars and bent them back into place with a metallic squeal. The cheering became a roar and she looked and saw herself, or rather Paragon, on the TV sets inside the concourse. Then the game announcer in his loud rumbling voice, declared, "Ladies and gentlemen, *iiiittttsss Paaarraaggonn!!'* She turned and could see out into the stadium and saw herself on the Sony Jumbotron.

All sixty thousand people stood up and cheered. The sound was deafening. Liza staggered at the sound of it. Her jaw hung open in awe. She saw how stupid she looked and gritted her teeth and stood up straight. They needed to see the Paragon strong. If she showed fear, they might show fear, and a stampede that size could kill a lot of people.

She waved and they responded by cheering louder.

She flew out into the stadium, up high by the scoreboard, and fist pumped the air, and the crowd somehow became even louder. Horns blared and whistled to join the thunder of thousands of people stomping their feet. Despite herself, she blushed. Her heart pounded in her ears, and she hung there in the air not knowing what to do next.

"Colonel, breech on the west gate." Liza gladly followed directions as she flew off to smash more robots. She found the thought of facing more killer machines a lot easier than facing that crowd. She found the robots lifting up the west gate bars, and she flew low and smashed into their feet. She arced up, outside again and turned back and began punching the things with ever increasing confidence. It hurt to hit them, like punching a wall, but after a bit her hands were numb to it. She liked the crunch sound they made when she hit them hard in the head, so she did. Over and over. They fired on her, mostly shooting each other in that close a space, and it was like boiling water splashing her, but adrenalin carried her on and she pounded relentlessly until she vaguely noticed they'd stopped fighting back.

"The Cheeseheads have stopped moving," said CyberSoldier over the com.

"Thank you, Captain Obvious," snarked Shokkusan, "but they aren't stopped. Not really. I'm picking up magnetic tickles coming off them."

"Magnetic tickles?" Liza wondered to herself as she stared closely at the nearest robot's face and then flicked it in the forehead, thus making a *klang* sound.

Shokkusan clutched her stomach as if she were queasy. "I'm feeling something wavy, like they're stockpiling power. I think they're going to blow! Take 'em down, *fast!*"

Explosions and noise erupted as the entire team poured on the firepower. Hurting the unmoving machines was far more efficient. Liza punched a few and broke off arms and heads, but she wasn't really destroying them. "Fly into them! Momentum is everything," John shouted in her ear. She obeyed by flying up and then, looping down, she hurtled into the chest of a robot with both fists out. It stung, but she flew right through it as it shattered apart. She did it again, picking up speed, and she smashed through two of them. She found it was like punching through a sheet of paper when she did it right, and she threw all her effort into it. It was also incredibly fun. She bashed three, then five, then eight at a time as adrenalin and testosterone pumped madly in her veins. She'd never felt this exhilarated. She let out whoops of joy and smashed with abandon.

Then, just like that, it was over. Metal and plastic debris were everywhere; hulks of robots melted and overheated at odd angles, others jerked and twitched and popped sparks from shorted out circuits. Scorch marks were burned all over the grounds. Car alarms bleated among the scores of vehicles destroyed. It made the parking lot look like a deranged Christmas tree. Slowly at first, then in a flood, people poured out of the dome. Some were panicked, some were grabbing souvenir rubble, and some took the time to kick the already destroyed machines.

Liza was watching the crowd emerge from the dome and trying to slow down her ragged breath and erratic heartbeat when someone called out, "Paragon! There he is! He saved us!" And the crowd surged towards her, thousands of faces all begging for autographs or kisses or who knows what. Liza didn't wait to find out. When the crowd came at her, she freaked and flew up high into the air.

The agents took over crowd management with the aid of the Chicago PD. "This is where you pick out a hot young reporter and give her a quick interview and then get the hell out of there. Otherwise, you'll be there for days doing clean up," said John. "Oh, and not bad for your first day. Enjoy the cheering. Tomorrow the lawsuits will pour out by the thousands. Mental duress, property damage, and on and on. The agents will handle it."

The next few hours were a haze as the team regrouped and returned to the airport to board their jets back home. Control kept informing them of various aspects of Internet espionage and counter measures he and his fellow computer jocks were engaged in as they shut down the bad guy's networks. Liza just shut it all out. With the adrenalin gone, she was overwhelmed and just wanted a shower and a nap in a bed with a big puffy comforter. She slept through most of the flight to New York while everyone else shared robot smashing stories like comparing catches after a day of fishing.

The Blurr stayed behind to help the clean up effort, because, according to Control, he was bored.

Liza blinked when they touched down and staggered, half asleep into the car that was headed back to headquarters. It was deep into the night when she stumbled to her desk. John was still there. He had ten full bags of fast food waiting for her. "I know how many calories that body needs, and I know you haven't eaten anything. Eat," he said. She had no idea she was hungry until he said it. Then she was ravenous.

As she polished off the first two bags and reached for the third she asked, "What happened to eat a carrot?"

"Just eat. Did they do a debrief on the plane?" John asked. Liza wobbled her head yes as she dug out more burgers and shoved them in her mouth like M&M candies. "Good. That means you're free until another situation pops up, unless the bosses want you to make the nightly talk show rounds. If they do, tell 'em to shove it. It's not quite last call yet, so Shokkusan and Cinaed will be around soon to drag you out for their post brawl bash."

"Unh Uh. Bed," Liza mumbled, her mouth stuffed with french fries.

John laughed. Liza thought it was weird to see her body laugh when she wasn't laughing. "This was an easy day for me. Usually the crises comes in threes."

"Your life is insane," she said with her mouth full. She found the Paragon's mouth was a lot bigger, and her super strength made the burgers squish like marshmallow when she chomped.

"That's why I want a vacation as you. Your life is quiet. Easy." John stole a fry. "Your friend is quite the talker by the way. She wants me, or rather *you*, back immediately. She's worried. But what she most wants to know is if you've found out yet whether the Paragon is a good kisser."

"Not on your life," said Liza, as she slurped down an oversized drink.

"I thought you were one of my fans?" he said in a teasing voice.

"I got over it."

Not long after, Liza was snoring in the office chair.

She was woken up after a few hours when John picked up a ream of paper, walked up behind Liza, and smacked her in the back of the head.

"*Ow!* What the fuck?" Liza yelled, clutching the back of her head, her eyes trying to focus.

"Time for bed. I need you to get into my apartment."

"You didn't have to hit me. That hurt!"

"You were shot a thousand times today. This was nothing. Besides, you're invulnerable. Ever try to wake an invulnerable tank?"

"I feel pain normally and *you* know it."

"Yeah. I just did that because it was fun. Come on. My place is on the top floor."

She muttered, "Jerk," as she followed him to the elevator. When she got inside, she crossed her arms and leaned against the far wall to get as far away as she could from John while still being in the elevator.

They went all the way to the top floor, which only contained a short hall, with five doors, two on each side, and one with a star at the end of the hall. John walked up to his star-covered door and waited. Liza remained in the elevator for a bit before walking over lethargically.

"Put your hand on the scanner," John said as he pointed at the blue panel next to the door handle. Liza obliged, and the door slid open with a series of clicks and a hiss. As the door moved away, it was revealed to be a half-foot of steel that looked a lot like a bank door. It had rods along the edges that had retracted. John walked in, "Lights," he said but nothing happened.

"Lights," muttered Liza and a small entryway was revealed that opened into a wide living room dominated by a glass wall that showed night lit skyline.

"Shades," said John, and Liza repeated the word. The glass walls dimmed to a neutral gray.

The furnishings were sparse: black leather couch, two matching arm chairs, art deco steel, a glass coffee table, and rug with a star emblem covering part of the hardwood floor. Kitchenette to the right, door to what Liza assumed was a bedroom on the left. Mementos were hung on the wall. The previous Paragon's uniforms were framed and hung above the faux fireplace. Medals and trophies filled black glass shelves. The walls were painted red above and blue below with a slow curving wave of a wide white stripe between them. "It's a nice place," she thought to herself, "if a bit cold and egotistical." Personal items were absent, she noted, along with anything welcoming. "Definite guy place," she thought. She also observed that it was immaculately clean.

"Maid, or do you dust with super speed?"

"Electrostatic filters scrub the air clean. No dust. I had a maid once. Turned out to be a double agent."

"Before or after you slept with her?" Liza asked sarcastically.

"After," he said seriously. John grinned, and Liza didn't like how she looked when John smiled.

"Anything I should be careful of?" she grumbled. "If this place is voice activated, I don't want to turn on any alarms by accident."

"No. All pretty simple. There is a code word for the alarms and the com system, but I want some privacy, so I won't tell you how to do that."

"How nice. Is there a bathroom in here?"

"Through the bedroom."

"Where are you sleeping?"

"In my bed. Why? Thinking of joining me?"

"*No.* I just assumed I'd get the bed and you'd get the couch or something. It's the gentlemanly thing to do."

"I'm not a gentleman. Even if I do play one on TV."

"Fine. I'll take the couch. Are there extra blankets somewhere?"

"There's a linen closet next to the bath. I have guest toothbrushes in the first drawer under the sink."

"Of course you do. How do you shave? I have a shadow of steel wool that could sand wood."

"There's a terawatt laser mesh razor under the sink. It only holds a thirty second charge and then takes all day to recharge, so I only shave in the morning. It works on my nails too. It's not easy to work, and it's insanely hot, so you might want to try a beard for awhile. When I want a haircut, I let Cinaed burn it into shape and then laser off the frayed ends. Hence the buzzcut. Not much else I can easily do except a mullet."

"Boo hoo. Poor little super boy."

"Speaking of bath stuff, when am I going to need the wing things?"

"Wing things?"

"The underwear pad stuff, for when Aunt Flo visits?"

"Oh. My. God. We are *not* having this conversation."

"I could always call up Gwen. I'm sure she knows. Two girls living together, probably on the same cycle."

Both of Liza's hands went up as she gestured. "*Just stop! Stop talking!* You're on birth control. You have about five days."

"Cool. You ever smoke? Because ever since I got your body, I've craved cigarettes. They do nothing for me as Paragon."

"I quit! Don't you dare ruin my lungs!"

John idly scratched the back of his thighs, "How do you shave the back of your legs? I can't see anything. I tried and nicked myself good. I'm not used to bleeding, and I don't want to bleed to death."

"You're not going to bleed to death from shaving. As for how, you just do it. Like flying."

"Great. You're going bohemian. Pants only."

"I do that all winter anyway."

"No wonder you're single."

"Leg hair has nothing to do with that, and how do you know I'm single?"

"Gwen. Push the go button and she's a fountain of trivia."

"Leave her alone! You have no right to interfere with my life!"

John shrugged. "You gave Kinny the cold shoulder. I have to live with that."

"You don't like her!"

"Maybe not. But did you ask me first?"

"I didn't *know* to ask you then. If I had known, I'd have asked and not messed up your relationship with someone you don't want a relationship with."

John threw up his hands, mocking Liza's earlier gesture. "Alright. I'll give you that point." John turned and headed off to the bedroom. "I'm getting the bathroom first. Your body can't hold its tea for damn. And it reeks. It needs a shower." Before Liza could say anything, he was through the bedroom door and had kicked it closed. Liza in turn flopped onto the couch forcefully enough to make it bang on the floor.

"Pig."

Liza laid on the couch, arms crossed, brow furrowed. She was in the queen of huffs, but long before John got out of the shower, she had fallen asleep.

The next morning John was banging around in the kitchen and Liza woke with a stiff neck and a groggy feeling from lack of sleep. She was covered in a comforter that John must have thrown over her. There was a pillow tucked under her head.

"You eat eggs?" John called out over the sound of a spatula hitting a fry pan. "I make a killer omelet. I can put in whatever you want. Just tell me what."

"Is that coffee I smell?" moaned Liza through droopy eyelids.

"Yeah, but it's a singles machine. You pick one of the packs in the cupboard, shove it in, and it brews for you. I used to leave my coffee maker running when I ran out for emergencies. After ruining four of them, I got this. Help yourself."

Liza shuffled over to the kitchen, wrapped in the comforter as if it were a bathrobe. She wrinkled her nose and sniffed her underarms. "Shower first." She shuffled in the other direction. She found the bathroom, like everything else, immaculate. She also found a magazine bin with girly mags next to the toilet. She nearly shrieked and leaped off the toilet when she noticed them.

John was eating his breakfast on the couch, watching the morning news when the lights turned red in the apartment and a klaxon sounded from speakers hidden in the walls. Liza appeared in the bedroom doorway, dripping wet, covered in a towel from her chest down. "Let me guess. Situation?"

John nodded. "Situation."

8

Six hours later, Liza had just finished cleaning up an overturned tanker truck of toxic something or other that had caught fire in Boston. It had burned off most of her costume and made her smell like moldy peaches. Liza had been on the scene first and was mostly confused about what to do. Control tried to help until the com link melted. Cinaed arrived later by black copter and with a wave of her arms, had the flames moving where she wanted them to go. She also made rude and suggestive comments about the few remaining pieces of the Paragon's costume. Nothing was hurt, other than Liza's pride. She flew back on her own to drive off the smell and avoid any more of Cinaed's incessant innuendo.

Paragon had a landing pad on the roof. There was a security door and private small stairwell that led down to the hall that contained the Defense Force apartments. Liza staggered down the steps. The Paragon body was fine and wide-awake, but she still felt like she'd missed too much sleep. She was relieved to find the apartment empty and immediately went in to have her second shower of the day. She found John's note on the coffee table after she was dried and dressed. "At the movies" was all it said. She tried reaching him on the com and couldn't.

Having nothing better to do, she explored the apartment. In John's closet she found five extra costumes, all-identical, all tacky. There was a drop chute next to the closet that said "hazard disposal," so she threw the remains of the old costume into it. She put the new suit on and turned on the com. "Control?"

"Yes, Colonel?" he chirped at once.

Now she wondered if he ever slept or rested. "Have we ever just hung out? Had coffee?" Liza asked, unsure of what she was going to say until she said it.

"No, sir," Control answered hesitantly, as if he expected to be yelled at.

"Well you saved my butt yesterday, and you've taken care of me for a long time. I think it's time I stopped taking you for granted. We're on the same team, so we should be friends… Right?"

"Yes, sir. If you say so, sir. That's understandable. Thank you, sir."

Liza found it interesting how nervous his voice was. "Where are you? I mean, where do you work? I'd like to meet you. In person, I mean. See your office."

Liza punched herself in the leg as she mentally berated herself: "Stupid! What if John knows where Control works?"

"Really? I mean of course, sir. I'm in sub basement thirteen."

"This building has basements? They aren't marked on the elevator," she thought, but she caught herself and said, instead, "It's been a long few days. Can you remind me how to get there?"

"Oh. You have to switch elevators. Go down to the garage level, then instead of going into the garage, go down the hall like you're heading for the gym. Go down past the gym doors, and it's on your right. Look for the green doors with the security pad. That elevator will take you down to any of the labs and facilities. We're on level thirteen with the rest of IT. You're cleared for all access except, level nine."

"Why not level nine?"

"That's classified."

"Huh. So there's secrets even from me?" Liza said out loud and then realized what she'd said. She mentally muttered, "Am I trying to give myself away?"

"A few secrets," said Control, the apology clear in his voice. "Permission to speak freely, sir?"

Liza hesitated. What had she stepped in? "Always. I mean I always thought you did. Speak freely that is. No need to be formal. Say what you want."

"Oh. Sure. Thank you, Colonel. Um. Can you give me a bit of time to clean up before you come down? I don't get many visitors..."

"That's it? Sure. No problem," Liza said with relief.

"Thank you, sir."

"It's Liz-eh-John. Just call me John, not sir."

"Yes sir. John. Sir."

Liza suppressed a giggle with some effort as she turned off the com. Robotic-voiced Control swallowed his emotions even when he was being urgent. It was funny to hear him nervous. It made him seem human. Duty aside, she decided he was a nice guy and was pretty sure John wasn't nice back.

"More evidence to not trust John," she said to herself. "I swear, everything John says irks me. It's like I moved back in with my brother. And I don't think he's going to fix this anytime soon unless I light a fire under his ass. To do that, I need to know more about him." She started poking around his closet and drawers again, not sure what she expected to find. Mostly she found stashes of videotapes and magazines. "I need to find out something other than his taste in porn." She sat down on the bed, trying not to imagine him pleasuring himself on it. "I need to make some allies too. Just in case this all goes south. More than it has." Liza felt better for having made that choice.

Liza changed out of the Paragon suit and found some black jeans and a faded red t-shirt. The only shoes she could find were a pair of black dress loafers and the god-awful Paragon snakeskin boots. She opted for slippers she found under the bed.

She had time to kill, so she made a coffee with the machine. It tasted like dishwater, so she poured it out. She wasted another fifteen minutes by idly looking through the kitchen pantry and cupboard drawers. She didn't find anything interesting. She stared at the clock on the wall and sighed, then she headed downstairs.

She found a coffee shop on the main floor and was distracted by the never-ending menu. Normally her coffee consisted of milk and sugar with a drop or two of the black stuff, but she was feeling adventurous today. Her town was too small for a Starbucks, so she'd never really had a choice before. If she had gone to one she'd never have been able to pay the prices. She discovered, to her delight, that any purchases went straight to her expense account, which was good, because as far she could tell, John didn't even own a wallet. She went for the most complex and expensive thing she could find entirely on the principle that she could, so why waste the opportunity? Whatever it was arrived steaming in a ridiculously large cup and looked like burnt sugar covered in whipped cream and smelled like cinnamon. Liza shrugged and sipped. It wasn't bad.

She tried to follow Control's direction, but got lost and wandered around until she found the right elevator. She put her hand on the blue pad and it chirped. A whirring sound followed and then the door opened with a ding. She entered and pushed the down button for thirteen but noticed the number nine was worn down from use. Must be a popular secret.

There was no music so she hummed to herself. There had been a hand sanitizing station next to the palm reader, and on the ride down she pondered if the Paragon was capable of spreading germs.

The door opened onto a wide hall. To the right was a wall of glass with an occasional vacuum-locked dock door. Beyond the glass, computer server racks were stacked in never-ending banks blinked in patterns that seemed to be both purposeful and random. To the left was a series of offices and storerooms of varying sizes. Cables in a rainbow of colors ran along the walls and floors and were bundled in columns that led into the ceiling. Whiteboards and some of the glass were covered with sloppy handwriting and geometric symbols done in dry erase markers. Someone was cleaning one of the boards somewhere unseen, but the acrid scent of cleaner filled the air. The air was cold, and the occasional person she spotted darted about were wearing thick fleece hoodies over their jeans. The ambient background noise from fans and beeping things made it difficult to concentrate. In short, it was chaos. A Yin to the Yang upstairs in the well-dressed and tidy agent control room.

From one of the rooms, Control wandered out in a flannel shirt, jeans, fingerless black knit mittens, and, of all things, furry Ugg boot knockoffs. He was rail thin, something she couldn't tell from the monitors. His hair, without the ball cap, was light brown hair and cut about two inches long. That made it stick straight up in all directions like a porcupine's quills. His features were slight and indistinct, but his chin was sharp. He wore hipster glasses that looked like they belonged in the fifties, and a blondish fuzz around his face indicated he either hadn't shaved or could never grow a proper beard. He was nervous, palms sweaty, and he wiped them on his jeans in preparation for shaking hands. "Colonel. Welcome to the lair."

Liza walked over to him, careful of the wires she had to step around, and handed him a plain, tall, black coffee. "I don't know if you like coffee, or how you take it, but here. It's black."

"I generally drink it cold and black. Thanks. This way." He gestured to the room out of which he had come.

Inside the cube shaped room was what seemed to be a hundred monitors mounted in a semi-sphere around a desk, each showing a different stream of data or video feed. A dozen keyboards, some stacked over each other like a church organ, an army of black mice, and a few joysticks were scattered around the semi-circular desk. A single small trash can underneath the desk overflowed with fast food wrappers and paper cups. Scattered everywhere like confetti, including on the screens of the monitors, were thousands of sticky notes in several colors, each filled with scribbled words or drawings. Dilbert cartoons were taped to several places. A dozen toys and action figures were scattered about the desk. A few of the characters were pure ribald cheesecake – buxom young anime girls with big eyes and clothing that was impractical for any purpose beyond pole dancing. Some of the figures were robots or armored suits carrying giant guns and giant swords. Liza gasped when she noticed a set of action figures of the team, including a fully articulated Paragon collapsed in an anatomically awkward position. Liza had the same figure. It had too many joints and would never stay upright unless you used the stand that came with it. Sticky notes had been attached to the figures with word balloons drawn on them to create a cartoon tableau. Paragon's note said, "Stand back, citizen, because I'm *Impressive!*" Cinaed's said, "I'm so *hot*. You must do me *now.*"

Control followed Paragon's gaze to the figures and a flash of panic flushed his face red as he rushed to sweep them up and dump them into a drawer. "Sorry, sir! I forgot about those. I use them for planning, but the jokes... a little kidding around the lair... stress relief... I didn't mean... Shit." He slumped against the table apparently expecting to be fired.

"At ease, son." Liza tried her best to sound pretentious and failed as she giggled. "Cinaed *is* hot."

"Oh, she is," Control stammered in relief then realized what he said. "Not that I would - I totally respect her sir."

"She has that effect on men. I've seen it many times."

"You aren't going to say anything to her, are you?"

"That you have a crush on her?"

Control blushed. "I don't have a crush. I just admire her a... lot."

Liza was surprised to discover his infatuation annoyed her. "It's always the pretty ones who don't need attention that get all the attention," she thought, "besides, Cinaed is clearly out of his league."

"Wait," she mentally chided herself, "everybody tells *me* I'm attracted to men out of *my* league, so what? Now I'm projecting? How fair is that?"

She said out loud, "So, Control, how do you keep track of all this?" Liza waved at the computers. "It gives me a headache just looking at one monitor."

Control warmed up instantly. "I've got this system. I code in key words to my search routines. They, in turn, pull important stuff from the periphery to the central feed, and conversely anything I flag as peripheral drifts back outward. I also designed the system to learn from my input. Sometimes it gets too focused and I have to reset it, but the system learns incredibly fast, so that's not a problem. I've got some presets for different kinds of missions, so it adjusts to the problem at hand. At any given time, there are up to eight other guys linked in manually doing the same thing on a parallel feed. The systems are averaged, so I have both AI and human intelligence reviewing the information stream. Plus, we can skim feeds off of backdoors we've installed into America Online and CompuServe. It gives us up-to-the-second input from people around the world. We have incoming feeds from the CIA, FBI, and the NSA as well. Combined, we have both intelligent and *semi*-intelligent sources at all times. If only we could figure out which was which! Hah!"

Liza understood some of what Control was saying, but he talked so fast, and the concepts were so abstract, he lost her almost at once. She just smiled as he talked and laughed when she realized he was joking. The smiles worked and encouraged his geekiness to blossom. He opened up even more, explaining everything about anything, pausing every so often to actually do his job, though Liza was unsure what it was he was doing. He would type something onto one of four keyboards using only one hand. He boasted that he was maintaining several chat windows while simultaneously sending commands to automated programs. All Liza could figure out was that he could move his hands and eyes at lightning speed without breaking his concentration. Occasionally, one of the monitors he interacted with would spew green computer code onto a black screen, and he'd respond with a flurry of nonsensical text. Then it would go away and be replaced by cable news. The more Liza watched, the more Control seemed to do at once. His ability to multi-task was beyond what any normal person should be able to do.

"Are you a power, Control? I couldn't follow any of this if my life depended on it."

He grinned a bit and ran his hand through his hair. "Sorta. I mean, I'm way WAY above the median IQ on several standardized tests, and I have an aptitude for coding in the 99th percentile, but it's not all me." He tapped his neck where a circular bump was visible under the skin. "Implants. I've got a computer chip in my head. It's the prototype for what's in CyberSoldier. Humans only use a portion of their brains. With my chip, I average about forty percent more brain activity then my norm. Connected to the external mainframe I can average around seventy-five percent. One doctor said my brain scan looked like a drag racer taking speed! I could go higher still if they lick the bandwidth issue. There's also a blood flow problem that kicks in when you approach that rate which is a downer. Brain cells get too hungry. I get the munchies for a week."

"Wow," said Liza, "That's… great… really…" The concept of a chip in her skull and a wire in her neck did not sit well with her. At all.

"Yeah. It's a *wow*. I have to go into shut down for three hours a night, or my brain starts hallucinating data. I only sleep about five hours a day anyways. Cat naps mostly, spread across all shifts."

"Did you want this? Did you know what you were getting into?"

"Yeah. You kidding? I volunteered! At first I was recruited for the Agency based on my aptitudes, but when they showed me this project, I had to get plugged in! It's a rush like nothing else! And I get to make a difference. It's good. Real good."

Something about his tone had Liza thinking he was quoting someone's brochure. She wasn't even sure if this was a bad thing, but someone having a chip put into one's head was too creepy for her to accept as something a person would want to do.

Bit by bit, Control got dragged back into his job as Liza watched and occasionally commented. Eventually, Control relaxed enough to joke around with her and not hide the snarky comments he sent back and forth to his nerdy cohorts. He told her about each of his teammates, and told a few stories he thought were colorful - but they were all pretty tame, even by Liza's dull life standards. It was clear these guys never got out, and several of them had never seriously dated anyone. She understood them too well. Until a few days ago, she was one of them.

"So what's your real name? You weren't born Control. That's a code name right?"

For the first time, he fell silent. Even stopped typing.

"Come on, Control. You know my name, and I don't know yours."

"I only know your code name, Colonel. I'm not privileged to your secret identity, Paragon, sir."

"Really. Guy smart as you? You know my social security number and my shoe size."

"I don't look at private information, sir."

"It's John West, and you know it. And I'm not asking you to tell me all your secrets, or to break any regulations. I just want to know your name. I think it's a wall between us. We work together every day. We should know who we are."

"Adam Czerwinski." He pronounced it sir-winsk-ee and was clearly ashamed of the ethnic sound.

"There. That wasn't so hard was it? And I promise not to tell anyone, Adam. Thanks."

"Same here, sir."

"It's John."

"Yes, sir. John, sir."

"You're cute when you're flustered," she giggled and then blushed when she remembered she was not in the right body for giggling or blushing. She turned around and played with a monitor so Adam couldn't see her face.

"Sir?"

"Um, Cinaed says that to me all the time. I just imagined her saying it out loud and then I said it. Heh heh. Stupid of me. I was trying to imitate her voice and I don't think I got it right. Sorry if that sounded weird."

"What's she like? In person, I mean? When she's not playing to cameras?"

"You figured out she does that, huh?"

"You all do it, sir." There was a beat. "John."

"I guess we do. Well, in person she's just like she is on camera. Pushy, confident, horny as a bunny, and fearless. But I think that's an act, too. I think she never stops being *on* - camera or no camera. You know what I mean?"

"I think so." Another awkward pause as Control looked at his shoes. "What's going on with you two? Are you guys still together?" Adam's voice pitched up a few notches, clearly concerned he was walking on thin ice.

"I have *no* idea what's going on," Liza answered truthfully. "I can tell you that she *does* care for CyberSoldier. You can see it in her eyes. I'm just not sure how *he* feels. There's so much metal in his face it's hard to read him."

"You won't tell her, will you? That I like her? I don't want anything to be awkward. And I know nothing will ever happen. But I don't want her to know."

"Of course not. Though personally I would have guessed you'd like Shokku. She's a bit more geeky and fun. And she looks like some of your figurines, here, except for the parts that are anatomically ridiculous."

"Yeah, but she's not a red head."

"Oh," said Liza, nodding as if she agreed, but she didn't. She didn't understand men at all and she was *really* tired of being one.

Not long afterwards, Liza found an opening to leave and took it, and Adam dove back into his work without missing a beat.

On the way back up to the apartment, she was overwhelmed by a feeling of being small and insignificant. She knew if she were in her own body, Adam would never notice her. No one ever did.

Once back in John's apartment, she went through his refrigerator and pantry. There was nothing to eat that said comfort - just utility food like protein bars that had no appeal. "What kind of single guy doesn't even have junk cereal?" she muttered aloud. Then she noticed her flip phone sitting on the counter. She'd forgotten about it. She flipped it open, called Gwen's apartment, and tapped in the code to check her answering machine messages. No new messages. Not unusual, but something about it bothered her. When Liza lived at home, Gwen would call her up at all hours and record the random thoughts that bounced around in her head. Even after they moved in together, Gwen kept doing it, sometimes calling from her bedroom while Liza was in the living room.

Liza punched in the key sequence that rewound and checked all the messages on the tape and found there were new messages, but they'd all been played. In fact, the tape was full. Gwen didn't know how to work the machine. John must have been checking them. She looked at her phone's history. He'd been answering her calls, too, and was making so many that she was out of minutes for the month.

He was using her life, and she didn't like that.

She went downstairs to the office to use John's computer. She logged into her AOL email account and shrieked when the voice said, "You've got mail." She read the last email. A few agents turned around from their desks at the noise, so she fake laughed out loud. "Ha Ha HA! Did you guys get that email picture with that thing? *Hilarious!* So funny. Ha ha." Then she sank as low as she could into her chair and wished she had the power to turn invisible.

She looked back at the email to be sure she saw what she'd thought she'd seen. There were several bank confirmations about wire transfers to her bank account with an obscene number of zeros attached to them. She called up her bank and convinced the teller she was her father. She had to recite her social security number and her bank account number before they would tell her anything. Then she nearly fainted. Her account had twenty million dollars in it. Two dollars she could believe. Twenty million? She double checked the account number figuring there was a mistake, but no, it was correct. She then discovered it wasn't one account, but a series of accounts that had been opened in her name. She dropped her phone. Twice.

It turned out that she could get all of this information online, and visions of cheeseheads running off with her money seemed far more scary than they previously had been. She had the teller walk her through how to check her bank accounts online. When she was certain she understood how things worked, she hung up and muttered to herself, "What was he doing?" as she rifled through the transactions.

Judging from the timestamps, he'd done most of this money dance in just a few hours, transferring most of it from a bank in the Cayman Islands. The name on the sending account was Gara Pon, which she stared at until she realized it was an anagram for Paragon. The hair rose up on the back of her neck.

She had an idea and typed John West into a search engine and hit pay dirt on the third listing. He was listed in a money magazine article speculating about the richest silent stakeholders in the world. Another link was an article from a year ago that listed him as the fourteenth richest man in the world. She searched, but she couldn't find anything else. She checked the bookmarks and browser history but both were erased. She poked around the computer and the desk, but she couldn't find anything that told her who John West was or where his money came from.

Then she remembered the outgoing calls on her phone. She checked each one by redialing them. Nothing interesting until the third one, which was answered by a woman with an accent that she couldn't place. It was English, but off. South African? Australian? The woman worked for an investment firm as some kind of secretary. She immediately apologized that a Mr. Dougherty was not in the office but would call him back as soon as he got back in, or she could give him his private number if this was an emergency. Liza hadn't had to say more than hello; the woman had recognized her voice, or rather John's voice. "No, that's fine. I was just curious what my current balance is," said Liza, trying to sound like a nonchalant John and not a terrified girl.

Liza's jaw dropped when she heard the response.

John was a billionaire.

Liza got off the phone and let the information wash over her. John was rich. Crazy rich. He had a nice place, but not crazy rich nice.

Her foot was tapping nervously. "Why did John dump a truckload of money into my name?" she asked herself. "Could it be a way to say sorry for all this hassle? No. *That* doesn't sound like John. Being sneaky *does*. What is he up to?"

John didn't carry a wallet or any ID. The Paragon suit had pockets, but there was nothing in them. Liza figured the agents and Control took care of him and he probably never needed money. Maybe they paid him a lot to be the Paragon and he never spent it and just invested it well. Could you get that rich that way?

Liza erased the browser history and cleared out the phone history. She went back to the apartment and put her phone back on the counter where she had found it. She no longer felt comfortable there, so she went back into the elevator and went down to the floor labeled "Commissary".

The commissary was a large cafeteria filled with agents and other support personnel, though it was segregated like a high school cafeteria as the agents all sat together. Liza grazed the selections and found fresh baked pretzels and gooey cheese. She added them to a tray with a chocolate milkshake and oversized chocolate chip cookies with giant chips. Then she added a piece of pie with meringue that stuck up a good three inches. She was the Paragon, right? It didn't matter what she ate, because her body could take it, right? Hard to say. John lied so often it was tough to figure out what was what. She looked at the pie and decided it was ok to eat it, regardless.

She carried the tray over to the register, and the woman smiled and nodded as she rang up her food but didn't ask for any money. Liza stared in confusion for a minute and then walked away with the tray and sat down. No one came by to tap her on the shoulder for not paying. Then she remembered the coffee and the expense account and smiled. She could get used to this.

She ate and found that her body was still hungry when her brain said she should be full. She got back up and found a heat-lamped pizza, took three different slices –

each with different toppings - and brought that back to her table. She ate that too. She still didn't feel full.

She started to wonder if this body got full.

She thought about it. She could recall being thirsty, but not hungry.

She thought about it some more.

The thirsty feelings were reactionary, like when she saw the coffee shop or rummaged around in the kitchenette.

"Maybe," she thought, "the Paragon body is like a dog with a never-ending food bowl that will eat until sick? But at least dogs salivate. They get hungry."

"What's up with you? I never see you in here." Liza started and then looked up to see Shokkusan holding a tray filled with fried chicken and what might have been dumplings in sauce.

"I was hungry. Had a craving for bad pizza."

"You? Really? I've never seen you eat junk food. And you bitch if any of us is snacking in the war room. Now look at you. Hypocrite." A bright blue worm of electricity crawled and snapped along the edge of her neck and shoulder.

"Interesting," thought Liza. "I hope Shokkusan zapped him when John told *her* to eat a carrot." Actually, Shokkusan looked like she would zap her now, or maybe smack her with her tray.

"Sorry. It's my dad." Liza said, "He had that whole 'Your body is a temple' thing going on. It's drilled into me…and I project…and I shouldn't. But at least it's in your best interests - got to be in good shape for crime fighting!"

"You are so full of shit, Colonel."

"Excuse me?"

"You heard me. Full. Of. Shit. What are you going to do? Fire me? I'd like to see that."

Liza felt her face flush and noticed people were watching. "Shokkusan, I'm sorry you feel that way, but I'm not your boss."

Shokkusan set down her tray and gestured widely. "You think I don't know? You own this whole place! You built it. Everyone here works for you whether they know it or not."

"When you say own…"

"Oh I know that we answer to the UN now, but we all know you and the other Para-goons were behind it. You may not officially run it anymore, but you're pulling the strings. I figured that out on day one. Go on. Deny it."

"So why are you still here then? If you dislike me that much?"

"Because you let me blow shit up."

"Is this really the place to have this conversation?"

"Where else am I going to have it? You don't bother hanging with any of us - Cinaed being the exception - and you don't approve of chitchat on a mission. Well Cinaed and I have said to hell with that. We're going to talk when we want to talk. You can keep on giving me the stink eye, like you did yesterday, but we're going to talk whether you like it or not. We aren't soldiers. And even if we were, soldiers kid around too."

Liza laughed. "You remind me of someone." Shokkusan didn't look or sound anything like Gwenifer, but she had her brass.

"What's that supposed to mean?"

"It means I respect people who stand up for themselves. And it's time I respected you. You did great work yesterday Shokkusan."

Shokkusan was taken aback. "You're in a rare mood. You're even using the honorific 'san'. Did Cinaed jump your bones?"

Liza wasn't sure what to say, so she tried guessing what John would say. "She's a beautiful woman and a good friend. But that's all. She's married. I'm in a good mood because we did a good job yesterday. The whole team. That simple."

Shokkusan leaned in and spoke so only Liza could hear. "Uh huh. Kin-kin tells me everything."

"Kin-kin? Well then she told you I turned her down when she came on to me in the hospital? Right?"

Shokkusan leaned back. She was speechless.

"Sit down," said Liza, getting an idea, "Let's talk. I know I can be a shit, but that thing, that attack at the bookstore? I almost died. That doesn't happen to me. Got me thinking. Got me thinking I want to change a few things in my life. One of them is how I treat my friends."

"Friends?"

"Well, teammates, at least. We could be friends. We should be friends. Sit down. Tell me the stuff I do that pisses you off the most, and I promise to work on fixing it."

Shokkusan tilted her head back and forth, staring at Liza's eyes. "You're serious."

"Serious enough. Can't promise you I'll become an angel, but I can try."

Shokkusan apparently believed Liza enough to sit down. Almost at once, Shokkusan cut loose, testing her. She pulled up grievance after grievance like a shopping list. The top of the list was her name. It was actually Shoko No Kimi, literally Shock Princess. Shokkusan was like Ms. Shock, and Shokkusama or even Shokuchan were acceptable. Shoku was insulting. She was the daughter of the former Japanese Prime Minister, and a legend in her country. Skipping the honorific not only insulted her, but her whole nation.

That was only the beginning.

Each point he ticked of was another rude insult or an egregious lack of respect that she took *very* personally. Liza flinched a few times, but mostly just nodded as she filed away mental note after note as to what it was really like to work with the Paragon. It didn't take long to verify the Paragon was a chauvinist pig of the highest order and an egotistical prick without peer. John seemed to consistently make Shokkusan stay out of his way except when he was in the mood to flirt. Liza came to understand that John didn't understand the word no and had stolen a few wildly inappropriate, and unasked for, kisses. Given the Paragon's strength, which was terrifyingly intimidating, it made Liza ill.

Liza swallowed a few times and tried to say it was all harmless joking around, using exactly the kinds of words her brother and his buddies used to say, and then Liza dropped a few of the same bullshit lines guys had used on her. She shuddered to see that they worked, and that she was making Shokkusan feel bad about being upset at things she *should* be upset about. Liza felt her stomach twist into knots.

Liza cut herself off. "You know what? Forget what I said. I'm just sorry Shokku*sama*. I never looked at it this way, from your point of view, and I was *way* out of line. As of today, it stops. You're my teammate, and I need to treat you like a peer and *not* a piece of meat." Liza's own anger at John colored her words and tone such that Shokkusan stared at her in stunned wonder. "You're my colleague. You have my back and I have yours. I can't risk you being hesitant because of the crappy way I've treated you. I'm sorry. For *all* of it. I'm an ass, and I understand if you don't forgive me, but I'm going to change anyway." Liza meant it, but as soon as she said it, she began to regret what would happen when she returned to her own body and John became the Paragon again. Shokkusan must have read the worry as sincerity because the anger melted from her face. It didn't last long. Liza spotted a few twitches of frustrated anger at edges of her mouth. Words weren't going to heal this rift, but it was a start.

They talked for another hour about empty things, but occasionally Shokkusan would challenge Paragon about something and remained tense until Liza apologized and promised to change and to never to repeat the offense. The tension in the air between them changed slowly to a radiated sense of relief. Liza felt an instinct to reach over and hug her sister-in-arms, but she resisted the feeling. Paragon was not one to hug out anything, and in this case it was decidedly the wrong thing to do. Eventually Shokkusan made an excuse to leave, and Liza let her go without opposition, but with one final sincere apology.

As Shokkusan walked away, Liza tried to imagine what she was like in high school, and couldn't. She tried to imagine her without the bright yellow costume, and couldn't. Liza had no idea who Shokkusan was, other than a proud woman who had been given no respect.

Liza sat alone for a time, lost in thought. Then she got up and made her way slowly to the apartment. She was worried she'd find John there and what she'd do to him. It was hard not to slap him, and a Paragon slap to her body would not be good.

In the short hall to the apartment, one of the doors was left open, and Liza looked in as she passed. The apartment seemed to belong to Cinaed since she was sitting backwards on a chair, and the chair was turned so she could lean on its backside and face the hallway. She was camped out watching the hall, wearing a bathrobe of some flimsy material that left nothing to the imagination, with an open bottle of wine in one hand.

"I see you," she said in a slurred, slightly loud voice. "C'mere! I wanna talk."

9

Liza debated which was worse: confronting John or confronting Cinaed. She chose Cinaed. "Talk about what? I'm kinda busy."

"You're always busy. Never time for anything."

"About the other day in the hospital…"

"You want me to *yell* in the hall? If *not* then get *in* here! Metal pants is out at the clubs in his *other* costume. It's just *you* and *me*!" Cinaed was shaking as she yelled. The wine sloshed in the bottle, and the air in the hallway noticeably warmed.

Liza decided she'd made a very bad choice and turned to leave, but then her mind filled with images of Shokkusan, and her gut told her this was the right choice to make. She walked into the room and shut the door behind her. If anyone knew who the real John West was, and what he was capable of, or up to, it would be Cinaed.

Cinaed seemed to be expecting the opposite and was more than a little surprised when Liza walked in. She sat up and took a swig from the bottle and then leaned back enough to clutch it in her lap.

Liza looked about the room in awkward silence. If she thought John's place was an austere bachelor pad, Cinaed's furnishings made John's place look warm and cozy in contrast. Everything was brushed steel or molded concrete, including the couch, tables, and chairs. There were no draperies, or carpets, or pillows, or upholstery anywhere to be seen. There were no decorations on the wall; everything was cold, utilitarian and uncomfortable. Then Liza figured it out – there was nothing flammable. Liza tried to imagine a life without comforters and pillows and was horrified. For the first time she felt a little sorry for the fiery red head.

"Well," said Liza swinging her arms, "ya got me. I'm here. What's so important that we need to talk?"

"Who the hell are you?" she growled.

"Excuse me?"

"You heard me. Who the *fuck* are *you*?"

"I'm –"

"*Rhetorical* question. Everyone knows who *you* are. I just want to know *who* the hell are *you* to treat *me* like a doormat? Huh? Well big F. U. Mr. Fucking Fuckface for being a *fucking fuck*!"

"Ah. You're *that* drunk."

"*Don't look down your nose at me!* Don't you *ever* do that to me!" The last of the wine began to boil in the bottle, and then the bottle shattered. "*Fuck!* Damn, damn fucking *hell*! Don't just stand there! Get me a towel Mr. super fucking *stupid*!"

Liza looked around and saw the apartment's layout was similar to John's, only smaller. She went through the bedroom and into the bathroom, where she found some very rough, strangely fibered towels. Passing back through the bedroom, she touched the bed. It was rock solid. Thin sheets of the same fabric as her bathrobe. She tugged on it. Strong fibers, and not at all comfortable. She felt even sorrier for Cinaed and decided that, if this was her own life, she'd drink too.

By the time Liza returned, she could smell burnt wine, which was a smell she found she recognized even though she knew it was new to her. There were some deep red scorch marks on the floor where the wine had vaporized. The glass shards from the bottle were dots and streaks of molten blobs that cooled as she watched into shiny little dark glass beads. Liza looked at the useless towel and tossed it to Cinaed anyway. Cinaed futilely mopped up the mess and then threw the towel aside with a drunken, weaving flourish.

"So," said Cinaed as she moved to the couch and put her feet up on the coffee table. Her legs were apart slightly, and she wasn't wearing undergarments. "So. Tell me. What do you see in that dumpy, lumpy, corn husker you've been dragging around lately? She's not your type. I know all of your types. Seen all of your types. She ain't one of them. What's the deal? Bored and slumming for a change of pace?"

Liza was taken aback like she had been punched. She took a half step to get her balance, feeling dizzy. Cinaed wasn't any worse than the cheerleader types back in high school, but it had been awhile since Liza had confronted such raw animosity. "I... I don't see anything in her. She's just a fan who helped me out. I'm just being nice and giving her the royal tour."

"I'll bet you are. Of your *dick*! I know how many fans you take up here to blow you. What I want to know is why she's still here? Is she *good* at it?"

Liza couldn't get the image out of her mind of girls going down on John. "You're out of line!"

"*Fuck you!*"

Cinaed hugged herself and shook as if an arctic breeze, instead of the sauna-like temperatures she was giving off, had blown through the silence.

Liza cracked her knuckles nervously and found they didn't pop. "There's *nothing* going on between us. Liza is just a sweet girl who got caught up in our screwy world."

"Sweet? You *are* banging her. What gives? Decided you like a lot more fat on the bones you jump on?"

"*Fuck you!*" Liza yelled as she kicked the concrete table, shattering it. Pieces ricocheted off the ceiling. "Liza is *not* fat. Just because she's not an anorexic bitch queen like *you* does *not* make her fat!"

"Did you just call me a *bitch*?"

"*Yes. I. Did.*"

Cinaed smiled. "You got me there. I *am* a bitch."

Liza took a deep breath. "I'm not doing anything with Liza. She slept on the couch."

"Nobody sleeps on your couch. Either they're in your bed, or they go out the door. What's going on?"

"How many times do I have to tell you? Nothing's going on!"

"Fine. You aren't fucking her. Something is *still* going on. You're Mr. Predictable. You do everything the same way, every time, but not anymore. These last few days you have totally not been you."

"I had a near-death experience. It changed me."

"Like *fuck* it did." Cinaed got up, went to the kitchenette, and popped the cork on another wine bottle. "Control called me, you know. All blah de blah blah bouncy happy puppy. Why? Because the master threw him a bone. I swear that boy calls me every day to gossip about something, enough so that I think he's as girlie as my sweetie, but still, this was different. You went down to his little geek playpen and patted him on the head. *You* don't do that."

Liza didn't like where this was going at all, and tried to change subjects. "He likes you, you know that? A lot. That's why he calls you. He has your action figure on his desk. He writes you poems. I saw one." Liza's face flushed as she realized how quickly she'd violated Adam's trust, throwing him under the bus to protect herself. She felt the bile rise in her gut, though given the Paragon body she was sure it was her imagination.

Cinaed waived her hand dismissively. "I'm just a centerfold to him. Him and every other dumb-ass male. You know? I ought to get staples tattooed on my belly, right here, so that I look perfect for my fans."

Liza's mood changed instantly from self-loathing to anger. "Well, if you didn't act like a whore and dress like a whore, maybe people wouldn't think you *are* a whore!" Liza couldn't believe her own mouth, but she had been thinking those thoughts for a long time. It felt good to say them, and it had the added bonus of completely derailing the conversation.

Cinaed put the new bottle down and sniffled suddenly. "Is that what you think of me? Is that what you've always thought of me? Whore? Is that who I am to you?"

Her eyes were steaming. Liza realized her tears were vaporizing as they formed.

"I'm sorry. I didn't mean that. I was angry. It's not true."

"Of course it's true." Cinaed got up and stalked back over to the counter. "I want everyone to want me, because I can't have anyone without killing them. Everyone except you. I don't want you. But you're all I can have."

Liza watched her fight back more tears, and all the anger vanished. Liza went over to Cinaed and held her from behind. Cinaed wrapped her arms around Paragon's without hesitation. She leaned her head back on Paragon's chest, then turned around to cry on Liza's shirt. Liza stroked her hair as gently as she could, but touching Cinaed was like holding a heated curling iron, and Liza bit her tongue not to cry out. After a few moments, Liza adapted to the heat and barely noticed the pain, so she held Cinaed tighter until she heard Cinaed wheeze, and Liza let up a bit.

When she was spent, Cinaed gently pushed Liza away and then sat down at the small dining table made of granite.

Cinaed looked Liza directly in the eye. "Who are you, really?"

"I'm a… fool for treating you so badly?"

"Cut the platitudes. I'm serious this time. Who are you? A clone?"

"No," was all Liza could think to say.

"You're not John. John doesn't hold me like that. He holds me, but not like that. He also drools over me, even when he's being a prick. You didn't grab my tits. You didn't even stare at me."

"I'm just feeling different since the attack," Liza stammered.

"Oh, give it up. You're a terrible liar." Cinaed got up and kissed Paragon full on the mouth. Then sat back down and watched the shock on Liza's face. "No. You're not him."

"Ok. I'm not."

Liza's hands drummed nervously on her thighs. There was no way out of this, and she was tired of hiding.

"I'm Liza."

"Liza? The dumpy girl?" Cinaed absently touched her own lips. "Ok. So what are you? Paragon four now?"

"No. John and I were forced to switch places. I'm him, he's me. He's in my body, I'm in his."

"What the hell?"

"It was that weapon of Dr. Psi's. He wanted to steal the Paragon's body using some beam thing, but I hit the old creep in the middle of it, and we ended up like this."

"You're a girl. A girl. In *his* body?"

"Yeah."

"Oh *fucking great.* Just wonderful. It so *sucks* to be me."

"It's not like I planned it! Or wanted it! All I want is my body and my life back. I want to go home!" It was Liza's turn to spontaneously cry. "But here I am, stuck and going on 'situations' and surrounded by strangers, and people are *shooting* at me and that *really hurts!*"

Cinaed just nodded and handed her the bottle of wine. "Welcome to the hero club."

Liza looked at the bottle. "Will this work on me?"

"Probably not. I never know if John is drunk or faking it. If you don't want it, pass it back."

Liza took a long drink before passing it back, "Ew. You have rotten taste in wine."

"Yeah? You fly like a drunk seagull," said Cinaed as she took a long drink and passed again.

"Fair enough," said Liza before taking a drink and passing it back.

They continued to pass the bottle in silence until it was gone. Liza nodded at the wine rack and Cinaed thumbed that it was Liza's turn, so she got the next bottle and opened it, fumbling badly with the cork screw. Her odd-sized body eventually broke off the top of the bottle. The break was clean, and there were no shards of glass, so she shrugged and took a drink. She sat back down and gave the broken bottle to Cinaed.

Cinaed looked at the jagged rim. "Unlike you, when cut, I bleed."

"Sorry," said Liza, "I'll get glasses."

"Fuck that. I'm a hero. We don't need no stinking glasses." Cinaed heated up the area around her finger and swirled it around the jagged edge, melting it smooth. Then she took a drink.

"*Ow!*" said Liza when her turn came and the hot bottle touched her lips.

"Suck it up, soldier," said Cinaed laughing.

Liza finished most of the bottle and found that she could, indeed get drunk. Cinaed said it wouldn't last long so either keep drinking or enjoy it while it lasted. Then Cinaed added, "So dish. Tell me the whole story. All of it. I need a laugh. The secret's out, so there's no harm in telling me the rest right?"

"Well… I guess not."

Once Liza started talking, she couldn't stop. Words poured out of her until she'd told Cinaed everything, leaving out only the the part where she spoke to Shokkusan. Cinaed did interrupt a few times, asking clarifying questions, and once to get another bottle, but mostly she just listened.

At the end, Liza watched the gears clank in Cinaed's mind. "Twenty million, huh. Why do you think he did that?"

"I waz going to ask you. You knows him."

"Nobody knows him. Not really." Cinaed got up, a little uncertain in her footing, but she steadied herself. She crossed over to a metal cabinet and pulled out a military ruggedized laptop. "His name's not John West, either. I don't know what his real name is, but he's got a bunch of them. I've heard Barry Richards, and Gene something. No one knows them all, as far as I can tell." She opened the laptop on the table between them, logged in, and then slid it over to Liza.

"Whaz thiss for?"

"Check your bank again. See if there's any more money or any less. Twenty million seems like an odd amount for a billionaire. Not that anyone knows what he's worth, but he's taken bribes from whole countries, and he's got a fortune for licensing his name and image. Don't believe his press, that it all goes to charity. No how, No way."

"You zound zoberer. Howz come I'm all woozy, and you ain't?"

"A lifetime of drinking practice. Now check your bank."

Liza fumbled around with the small keyboard, her big fingers having a lot of trouble. "Don't bang so hard," said Cinaed, "It's a tough little box but not Paragon proof."

"K. 'm Tryin'." Liza was reduced to single finger peck typing. "Uh oh." She typed again. "Yeah. I'm locked out of," hiccup, "my account. Pazzwordz changed."

Cinaed looked at the screen, "Change it back. There's a password reset option that goes to your email."

"Huh," Liza said, looking at Cinaed. "Didn't figure you for a comm... compooter perzon." Liza typed some more and her brow furrowed as she tried to concentrate. "I'm locked out of my emails thingies. He's changed all my passwords? The *fuck*! How did he even know all this? He's me, but he doesn't know this stuff! How did he even know my bank account?"

"He has an army of hackers, and he has your purse with your driver's license in it. Not rocket science. The question isn't how, it's why."

Liza tried to clear her head, and the madder she got the quicker the alcohol seemed to burn out of her system. "Why? What do you mean why? Oh. You mean why did he do this to me?"

"No. I mean why do it at all. Why take over your personal accounts unless he plans to keep them?"

"I thought that, too. Or that maybe he wanted to frame me. Make it look like I work for Dr. Psi."

"Why?"

"I dunno? So I wouldn't tell our secret? He threatened before to frame me if I talked."

"If he wanted to threaten you, he'd show you what he did, not secretly lock you out."

"He's not going to give my body back, is he?" Liza pinched the headache forming at the bridge of her nose as she leaned back. "But he can't hide. I know where he lives, and where I live."

"Stupid girl. He could run off to South America, or any country that owes him favors."

"Don't call me girl. You're not that much older than me."

"Fine. I'll just call you Stupid."

"That's better. But if he's in my body, I don't have a passport and those other countries don't know him in that body. So he's stuck, right?"

"Heh. Maybe I won't call you stupid. Anyway, he does a lot of his business without ever meeting in person, to hide his Paragon identity. He has an army of intermediaries, and all the agents would respond to emails and such. He still knows all of *his* passwords. He can correspond as Paragon."

"Crap. He could do anything. Call Control for me! Could you? John told me he was at the movies, but that was ages ago, and he's changed my accounts since then. I need to see where he is. Now."

"Why don't you call him? You tamed him. And you're Paragon. You're his boss."

"John doesn't know I'm on to him yet. If John checks up on me, it's better he has less of a trail back to me."

"Nice paranoia. Now you sound like one of us." Cinaed picked up an earpiece from the coffee table and came back. She made a shushing gesture. "Control, love, are you up?"

Liza couldn't hear what Control said, but Cinaed smiled.

"I have a little prank to pull on Paragon. He's been so stuck up lately, I wanted to get him back a little... No, nothing mean... I'll keep you out of it... I just want to put a blow up doll in his bed with Tigress's name on it... Yeah, that cat lady from China he likes... Yup. Shokkusan thought it up, but she chickened out... Paragon? Don't worry about him. He's here with me passed out drunk. I just want to know where that girl-toy of his is, so she doesn't spoil it. That Liza girl... Yeah. She's been sleeping on his couch... Oh, so she's not in the building, huh?" Cinaed whispered to Liza, "John has a building pass with your name on it and it hasn't been used in the building since this afternoon." Then to Control, "Any chance you can find her just to be sure? I don't know, put a trace on her credit cards?... Sweetie, you break laws for us all the time, and I'd be *ever* so *grateful*." Cinaed turned on the lusty voice, and Liza instantly felt sorry she'd told her that Control had a thing for her. "Great. Call me back when you know where she is. I don't want to move until I know."

Cinaed said to Liza, "He's thinking too hard about it, and I'm not lying well."

Cinaed said to Control, "Ok. Fine. The truth is I want to take Paragon upstairs and *use* his apartment for a bit. In *private*... Yes you should be embarrassed. I *was* trying to protect you, but you wouldn't let it go. Look, she's a civilian. She'll never know you checked up on her... I'll make this up to you. Promise." Cinaed rolled her eyes. "Don't be that way. If I can cheat on Cyber, why can't I cheat on Paragon?... Yeah. I just implied what you think I implied."

She rolled her eyes for Liza, "Men!"

Then she said to Control, "Well, you'll never know unless you try. Why wouldn't I be interested in a handsome young man that tries so hard to take care of me?" Cinaed made a gagging gesture, and Liza felt like dirt. "That will work, love... Perfect. I'll be busy, but leave the headset on answer. Make it flash, and I'll pick up." Cinaed took the piece out of her ear and set it on the table. "He has no idea where your body is, but if your credit cards get used, he'll know instantly. He's also flagged your driver's license, in case his jerkness uses it for an ID at an airport."

"This is all so crazy," said Liza, now feeling completely sober, but a little nauseous. "Why *are* you helping me?"

"He treats me like I treat a vibrator. I deserve better. And if he's run off on us, that sneaky little bastard is going to pay. If any of us were to quit, he'd ruin our lives. He makes no secret about that. He deserves the same."

"You make him sound like a mob boss."

Cinaed shrugged. "There's a difference?"

10

Cinaed and Liza ransacked Paragon's place. It started out innocently as a check to see if he had come back, and when it was clear he hadn't, it became a forensic investigation to see where he might have gone. At least that was Liza's intent. Cinaed was just seemed to be digging for dirt.

They systematically emptied his dresser, his closets, and the medicine cabinet. After Cinaed found a few old magazines and a sock from another age, she took to incinerating John's porn as she found it. When Liza came into the room she was assaulted by the smell and wondered why the smoke alarm hadn't gone off. "Honey, we disconnected those a long time ago, in my apartment, and this one. It gets too noisy when I visit," Cinaed gave her an exaggerated wink that made Liza gag.

Liza took on the rest of the apartment, checking the couch, the kitchen, more closets, anything. Her snooping before had been casual, but this time she left no stone unturned.

They both came up empty.

Dejected, both women slumped onto John's couch and compared notes. Cinaed had been here many times, but had never stayed long, and the apartment never changed. Paragon never let anyone stay long in his place, at this point, Liza may have set the record.

All of Cinaed's stories with Paragon led to sex, and Liza's face twisted up in disgust whenever Cinaed started down that road. She was slow to figure out that Cinaed found it funny to make her squirm. The one story that stood out, though, was about the Paragon costumes that were framed and hung on the wall above the fireplace. They were there now, to either side of the wall-mounted TV, staring at them. The one on the left looked more like an army uniform with a few stars added to it. The other was garish, bright colored, skintight, and it had a cape. The story, though, was that Cinaed had noticed one of the frames tilted out once, like a door, but before she could look behind it, Paragon slammed it closed with super speed. He wasn't anywhere near as fast as the Blurr, but he could put a cheetah to shame with ease, so she saw nothing. Cinaed had tried to look behind the cases on other occasions, but they wouldn't budge. She was sure she had imagined it until she said it again just now.

"Can't hurt to check," muttered Liza, as she got up and crossed over to the one on the left. The shadowboxes stood out a few inches from the wall, and they were made of dark metal, but there was a square of black plastic on the side of the frame against the wall at the bottom. Liza touched the panel, and it dimly lit up red, like a light through dark glass. The light was oval shaped and faded out when her hand moved away.

"Huh," said Cinaed, as she looked over her shoulder. "Try your finger. Hold it down."

"Like a finger print scanner?" said Liza as she touched it. There was a soft click, and the shadow box swung slowly out to reveal an indentation that contained a safe with a keypad.

The other shadowbox was the same. Same scanner, same type of safe behind it. They tried a few guesses at the combination, but failed. The safes' surfaces were smooth, which gave Liza no purchase to try to pry them open by force. Cinaed guessed she could burn through it with enough concentration, but decided that much heat would probably destroy anything inside.

They stared at the safes for a time, and then, having nothing else to discuss, Liza blurted out, "I just don't understand this. Why would he want to quit being Paragon? He said he wanted a vacation, but I'm starting to think he doesn't want to go back. Ever."

Cinaed shrugged. "He's a private guy, and this is a very public job. He fights tooth and nail to keep himself a mystery."

"So why the hell did he write an autobiography? Then do a book tour? That doesn't fit at all."

"Oh, it does," said Cinaed shaking her head. "There were several gossip books on the stands, and he always wants to control the message. Ever heard of Briar Books? They tried to publish a tell-all book about his love life written by this reporter he briefly dated. He bought the entire company in a hostile stock takeover and then drove them out of business. He pulped every copy he could and then sued anyone who mentioned it into silence. He did it all through shell companies and lawyers. Clean media kill. He even had the book destroyed in other countries by calling in a few favors with heads of state. People will do a lot to gain his favor."

"That's insane! He's got that much pull?"

"Haven't you been listening? He doesn't just own this team. He probably owns a few *countries*."

"So again. Why quit? He's got everything."

"Except privacy. Everyone knows who he is. He's rockstar famous, too. He picks his nose, and you can be sure it'll be front page on a tabloid somewhere. It's like being a fish in a fishbowl with millions of people watching you. It's a rough way to live."

"Is that why those guys quit?" Liza asked, pointing at the picture frames holding the suits. They were still swung open, revealing the safes, but Cinaed got the meaning.

"Them? No. The one on the left? That was Paragon One. No one knows where he came from. He just showed up one day in the big war, World War I, to oppose the Kaiser, and he stayed around doing this and that and eventually helped the Allies in WWII in a big way. He was the hero's hero. Loved by everyone, revered, almost worshipped, but he came out of that last war broken, shell-shocked. Never heard if there was a reason beyond the obvious, that war is hell. His persona inverted, he became jumpy instead of confident, easily angered instead of always smiling. He went from loving crowds to avoiding people altogether."

"That wasn't in the biography," said Liza.

"Of course not. They also don't tell you that in the end he'd lock himself in his home for months at a time refusing to speak to anyone." Cinaed took a long sip from yet another wine bottle she'd procured, "But it was the one on the right, the second Paragon, that talked the first into quitting. He campaigned for it. Met him at rallies, sent letters, all kinds of stunts. Said he wanted to be the next Paragon. Freaked the first out, but somehow the second wore him down and won him over."

"But," Liza interjected, "that makes no sense. You don't just get up one day and tell an outlier, 'Hey hand over your powers, I want a turn.' That's crazy."

"Actually, you'd be surprised. People will ask for anything. I met this waitress once who asked if I could give her a suntan in the middle of dinner. She was serious. But you're right, this was different and weird and the second was a little crazy. We all are. Sane people with superpowers find ways to make money or make their life easier. To put on a costume and be a hero takes a special breed. Me included, though I never had a choice in the matter. I was raised in this lifestyle; my powers were too dangerous for anything normal." Cinaed finished the bottle and rummaged around for more before coming back and continuing as if she hadn't paused. "I think it ties back to the manifesto Paragon One wrote. Inspired a lot of costume craziness, but it was meant to rally soldiers."

"That one I know. It's in the forward of Paragon's biography. 'Do what needs to be done and do not doubt that you are the one to do it. It is not power that defines the mighty as heroic, it is how heroically the might is used. Each of us is a candle deep in the night, and together we make a blazing light, but if we fail to make that light, then we deserve the darkness that consumes us.'"

"You are a geek. But yeah." Cinaed got up and decided to make coffee for each of them without ever asking. She kept talking from the kitchenette. "That little speech from the *Post* has been reprinted over and over. It did some good, but it also spawned a cult called the Lights. A bunch of wannabes who worship heroes."

"I thought they were a charity?"

"They are now. They didn't start that way. Paragon Two was their president at the time. Willy Drucker, pure beatnik. He hounded the Paragon for more quotes and wisdom. Personally, I think Paragon had a speechwriter, but regardless, he thought they were all loons that missed the point by a mile. Then, out of the blue one day, he sat down with them and asked them to do something with themselves. Just like that, they reformed overnight. They got off their asses and started building homes for the homeless, supporting veterans, stuff like that. Paragon started to publicly support them and raise funds for them. That fell apart when some of the founding Lights were accused of being communists and the organization was torn up in the red scare. They reformed later, with very few of the old ties. Willy was on the patriot side. He left and never had anything to do with them again."

"None of this was in the biography. It just starts off with Paragon Two as a small-town bartender."

"Well, after the Lights he was nothing. I don't know where he ended up. Bartending makes as much sense as anything, I guess. All I know is that was when he started asking Paragon One to pass on his powers, the Paragon avoided him like the plague. But he must have gotten through, I guess, because the Paragon started talking to him. Only person he'd let into his skank pad of solitude. Eventually, he gave Willy the power and dropped off the face of the earth. I heard he became a monk in Tibet, but I don't believe it. I think he sucked on a .44 until he fell asleep forever."

Liza shuddered at the image, shaking it out of her head. "But how did it happen? How did he pass on the powers?"

"Honey, ain't nobody knows, state secret, and many people have asked. You know more than I do, since you're Paragon now. What's more interesting is how Paragon Willy turned into Paragon John."

Liza accepted the coffee as Cinaed walked back and sat down. Cinaed looked exhausted. Deep circles loomed under her eyes. The alcohol's effects had burned out of the Paragon body fairly quickly once Liza stopped drinking. She felt fine, while Cinaed looked like she was suffering the ill effects for both of them. "Alright," said Liza after sipping a bit, "tell me how Two became Three."

"The government hated Two. He hated them more. He worked with them sometimes, and against them at others. Pick a day, spin a spinner, and that was Willy's political opinion for an hour. He was a complete loose canon. He became a hippy, but other times he was rah rah anti-communist and did the dirty stuff that needed to be done for Uncle Sam. Eventually he got sick of America altogether, something Nam related. Then he started the idea of the UN having an independent super soldier program to enforce the peace between nations. It was a mess, though. He was as bi-polar supportive and combative with the UN as he was with the US. He was just trouble. The Left called him a sell out, and the Right called him a traitor."

There was a pause while Cinaed asked for aspirin, and Liza checked and found none. Cinaed massaged her temples as she continued, "So along comes our John. Or whatever his name really is. Paragon Three. I've heard dozens of conflicting stories about his life before. Old money rich kid. New money rich kid. A Marine. A Congressman's kid. An entrepreneur. A real estate agent. Whatever. He was connected, and the right people liked him. Nixon got the White House, and, bang, a week later, John's the new Paragon. Willy vanishes. Probably taking a dirt nap in Arlington."

"Everything changed at once. John created the Agency out of a mishmash of support teams. Then he went out and ended 'Nam. Then he added a few more heroes to his team and reversed the mess Korea was in. Suddenly everyone that wasn't a socialist liked him. He was a guy who got things done. He campaigned for Nixon and got him re-elected, despite all that impeachment talk. *Every* election ever since, *whomever* he backs gets elected. He became the kingmaker. In exchange, he gets *whatever* he wants."

Liza was almost shaking. What Cinaed was saying ran counter to anything she read in the papers or heard on TV. "Wow," was all she could say for a time. "John wants to walk away from that? Who walks out on that much power?"

"No one. My guess is he wants to keep doing what he does without having to be the Paragon. Be the great and powerful Oz behind the curtain. He hates missions, especially rescue operations. He'll pull people out of floods and mudslides and smile while the cameras are running, then tell the survivors they were assholes for living on a flood plain when the cameras go off. He added us to the team so he didn't have to do as much."

"No, no, no. This isn't adding up. He sounds like he's a control freak. Why let me run around in his body without controlling me, too? Why run off with my life?"

"That's what I'm wondering," said Cinaed. "*Exactly* what I'm wondering. I bet he's out there right now figuring out how he can control you. You have family? People you love?"

"Oh! Gwen! *I've got to get home*!" Liza stood up so quickly she was hovering in the air.

"Sit down." Cinaed tugged on Liza's pants. "You're not doing anything in that body. It's your word against his. He's got a lot of allies who'd rather be enemies. You tell anyone you're not him, and you've got a world of trouble coming at you. And a world of trouble coming at *him*, now that he's in your squishable body."

Liza slowly settled back down, but the gears were turning in her head. "What if…What if the Paragon can't change bodies?"

"I don't follow. We have three of them."

"Yeah, but what happened to them afterward? All of the Paragons look the same, except for their costumes. It's their personalities that change. What if the body stays the same, but it's the mind that changes? If so, what happens to old bodies and minds? You think they're dead. Maybe they are. Maybe the old Paragon's mind gets erased by the new one? Maybe the old body is left with no mind?"

"Then John would never pass it on," said Cinaed, thinking hard as she rubbed the bridge of her nose. "He wants out, I'm pretty sure, but not enough to die over it. That's a pretty crazy theory, though." Cinaed stopped focusing on her headache, and her eyes took on a clarity that suggested she didn't think Liza's theory was all that crazy.

Liza was still troubled. "There's a problem with my theory. Why didn't John tell me how to switch back with him? He probably doesn't care if I get hurt. Why not switch back right away? Something else is going on. How old is this freaky Dr. Psi?"

"Old. He was a Nazi scientist that experimented on prisoners. Real sicko. We hunt him, have a few mix-ups, he escapes and stays hidden. Turns up all around the world doing bizarre mad science stuff. Had his hand in a lot of things."

"Maybe he had help not getting caught."

"Are you serious, Liza? Paragon, more than anyone, hated him. He declared Doc Psi public enemy number one."

"The Paragon stops wars and controls whole countries, but this one guy just runs around free?"

"Liza, you can't be serious."

"Think about it, Cinaed. A mad scientist who can switch people's minds into other bodies. A guy who runs around for years and never gets caught. He should be what, around seventy? Older? Then you add a Paragon who wants to quit and become the guy behind a curtain?" Liza's coffee cup was empty, which was good because her hand was shaking as she talked.

Cinaed put her hand on Liza's, steadying her. "You're telling me they worked together? Staged this? That's stupid. Why would John want to be a decrepit old thing?"

"Um," said Liza, thinking quickly as she talked, "maybe it was temporary? Maybe they'd do it twice? Make a big deal out of the switch, and then Paragon captures Dr. Psi and carries him away. Then they switch John into another body when no one is looking."

"Too risky for John. He'd be helpless. The doc could just kill him."

Liza sighed. "Yeah. That doesn't work."

Cinaed tapped her lip with her fingers, "Ok, so let's play with this some more. Let's say you're right, and this was staged. You weren't part of the plan."

"Yeah. I was a mistake. No matter what's going on, that part was true."

"So what would John do? For some reason, he won't talk you into switching back. What else can he do? Find the Doc and make him switch you back?"

"Why would the Doc do that if he's not getting the Paragon body?"

"Money? Power? I dunno," said Cinaed. "Moreover, why not switch bodies himself? He's ancient, get a new model." Cinaed covered her mouth in surprise. "Oh shit! He has! He wears masks and helmets a lot, but Doc's always looked young in all of the dossier pictures in his file. And anytime I've seen him, he's never looked so decrepit. That's why we can't find him. He jumps bodies."

"Money," said Liza, snapping her fingers and then wincing at the sound because it was as loud as a gunshot. "John has money. Lots of it. Lots of secrets, too. All in his head. The Paragon's body is nice, but it's only part of the Paragon's power, the rest is in John's head. If Dr. Psi took the Paragon body, he wouldn't know the secrets John knows. Look how much trouble I've had and John's *been* helping me. The Doc would get found out. But if John helped the Doc be Paragon, no one would find out. Doc gets the Paragon and the secrets, John gets a new body and keeps his money. That was the deal. I'm sure of it. Some parts I don't get, but that's the core."

"To paranoia!" Cinaed toasted her. "You need it in this job. People fear anything they can't control, and people are always jealous of power. So we freak people out. Politicians have it easy compared to us."

"I like this side of you," said Liza.

"What do you mean?"

"You're talking to me like I'm a person, instead of talking at me. You come across as this loud brash thing, but that's not you at all."

"And you're smarter than you look."

"Thanks, I think." Liza set her coffee cup down. "So now what…"

"Sleep. Even with the caffeine I can't keep my eyes open. We tackle whatever's next in the morning."

"I'm not sleeping here alone," said Liza. "What if he comes back?"

"You can sleep on my couch. Bring some pillows and blankets. I don't have any you'd want to use. And when Cyber sneaks in, pretend not to notice him."

"Is there any part of this that isn't going to be awkward?"

"Nope. Speaking of awkward, I should set the two of you up! It would be perfect. He's a perfect gentleman, and he just wants a lady in a man's body, and you only like men."

Liza's face went white.

"You're fun to tease." Cinaed slapped Liza on the shoulder and got up. "Sleep time. Come on. Before the world falls apart again."

They slept only a few hours before the team was awakened by a typhoon emergency warning hitting the Far East, but it turned out to be a false alarm triggered by a readiness exercise. The team members cursed under their breath at Paragon for making them fly half way around the world for nothing. Liza knew she had nothing to with it, but she felt awful anyway. She also caught a bit of jet lag and felt like she had the flu. After time zone changes and debriefings, three days passed before they were back home.

Liza had no opportunity to talk to Cinaed in private during the trip, so she kept up the pretense of being the Paragon the whole time, with Cinaed carefully giving her guidance. Liza bluffed with a sullen orneriness that was only half faked. She wanted to know where John was and what he was up to, but he was silent and unreachable.

Toward the end of the trip, Shokkusan had started giving her odd looks, and Liza just knew that Cinaed had told her everything. It angered Liza and made her more nervous, but there was never a time to confront Cinaed about it without being overheard.

Liza decided to corner the two of them during the layover in Dubai because CyberSoldier and Blurr were taking a different flight. They were being diverted to a peace-keeping mission in South Africa that wasn't going well. Something to do with the newly elected ANC, but Liza missed most of the briefing because of jet lag sleepiness. She was sure it wasn't really jet lag, because she doubted the Paragon could get jet lag, but the symptoms persisted nonetheless.

As they boarded the private jet, Control announced that they were being diverted to the gulf coast. Tropical storm Henrietta wasn't quite a hurricane, but it still did a hell of a lot of damage on some small islands in the Caymans. Briefings followed on the flight, and Liza fell asleep only to be awakened by the landing gear deploying. They'd landed in Florida to pick up relief supplies that Liza and some helicopters carried in. Shokkusan and Cinaed took boats and dealt with power lines and fires but mostly sat around or talked to news crews while Liza flew people and equipment and supplies from one place to another. It all looked the same to her, and she was kept moving so she had no time to think.

Blurr showed up on the third day, but it changed little. He moved so fast he could run across the water's surface, but he kicked up a huge wake behind him so the few times Liza was near him, all she got was wet. She tried to be social with him, but he never stayed in one place, and he could only be understood by Control, who had special software to record, slow down, and playback what he said because he talked so fast. Every conversation was filled with delays and pauses, like talking through an interpreter, and most of the time Blurr had no patience to answer, so Liza gave up.

The agents that Liza met were all "Yes, sir" and, "No, sir," and nothing at all like chatty 33 and 34. The only human communication she had was with the people she rescued, but they spoke broken and heavily accented English. The emergency relief workers that assisted were too busy to chitchat, but they always found time to ask for an autograph if she stopped them.

Liza was surrounded by people, and yet she had never felt so alone.

The morning of the sixth day, Liza was flipping through a clipboard of things prepared for her that needed doing. Cinaed and Shokkusan had gone home, and only she and Blurr remained behind, doing clean up. She was sipping phenomenal local coffee to try and counter a scant five hours of sleep. She'd learned that the Paragon did get tired, especially when the body didn't eat but did strenuous work. She'd taken to downing protein bar after protein bar for the last few days, but it hadn't been enough.

By the time she'd finished her coffee, the sky had gone from wispy clouds to a torrential downpour. She was in a canvas tent, and the rain pouring down outside made a relentless drumming roar. It was loud enough that nothing else could be heard without a shout. So when it suddenly went quiet, Liza jumped, which almost caused her to fly, but she caught herself and only hovered to the top of the tent. A mocha skinned man in a black Kevlar body suit was standing there vibrating.

"Blurr?" Liza asked, as she landed.

"What's. Going. On."

His mouth would go out of focus, and his words had an echoing sound, but he was understandable. On the folding table between them was a metal pyramid shaped device with a green light on it. It hadn't been there a moment before.

Liza recognized this from her dealings with John. "Privacy field?"

"Yes."

"What do you mean *'what's going on'*? You want the mission brief?" she asked as she waved the clipboard.

"On. With. You. No. Cameras. Relief. Workers. Here. We. Are. Still. Here. Why."

Each word seemed to be an effort, like an opera singer holding a single note, and his words had a vibrato sound to them. "We're here because this is our mission. Agent One selected us, and he hasn't told us we're done here. Is there something I'm missing?"

"You. Are. One."

"One of what?" Liza was fascinated that Blurr could understand her, and she tried to get a sense of his features, but the longer he remained, the more he'd vibrate and blur the image. It was like looking at someone in a fog.

"You. Are. Agent. One."

"Me? I'm Agent One?" Liza's eyes matched the confusion in her voice.

"What. Is. The. Real. Mission."

"Um, this is it. Helping people. It's what we do."

"You. Are. Toying. With. Me. Punishment."

"No. No, I'm not. We're just helping people. You're doing a good job, by the way. Thanks."

"You. Know."

"Know about what?"

"Yes. I. Am. Still. Smuggling." The longer words were harder to make out, but Liza was pretty sure he'd said "smuggling" and not "smut. lying," which was what it had sounded like.

"Ok. Um…You're right. I do. Known all along. Yup. Did you think you could keep it a secret from me and my cleverness?" Liza tried to sound intimidating and knew she had failed.

"My. People. Need. Work."

"And that justifies smuggling?"

"Only. Bring. Honest. Men."

"Right, because only honest men are involved in smuggling." Liza thought she was doing better with her snarky voice.

"They. Are. Just. Farmers. Punish. Me. Not. Them."

"Oh," said Liza, the light bulb going off in her head, "immigrant smuggling. You're smuggling people…across the border. And you did this before. And you got in trouble for it." She was making up what she was saying on the spot, trying to think fast. If John knew about this, he'd use it against him, so that's what she had to do.

"Please. It. Is. Over."

"Yes it is. Good choice. You don't do it again. Nope. And tell you what. You remain loyal to me…and I'll not do anything about this. We're even. Loyal. Even. Deal?"

There was a long pause, which for the Blurr must have seemed like an eternity. Liza thought he was looking for the catch, the small print that's always there when you make a deal with the devil.

"Deal."

"Good. Good talk. And since the relief troops have arrived, I think you're right. It's time to go home." There was a whoosh of wind as the sound returned, and the device and the Blurr were gone. Liza added to the wind, "Good talk. Let's do this again sometime." She shivered, though she wasn't cold.

She sank into the canvas chair. The Paragon's body barely fit into it. She looked about the tent and listened to the rain. "I'm Agent One. The numbers are ranks, and I'm *number one*. The guy that sets the agenda. Paragon runs the Agency."

She leaned back a bit to take it in, and the chair broke under her, but before she hit the ground, she was hovering in the air. She decided to just hover, slowly spinning while she thought. "Someone is still running the Agency, but I haven't been doing that, so is there another Number One, or is John still in charge somehow? Easy answer is that it's John. So somehow he is running the Agency while in my body?" She thought back to every meeting she had with the agents and what Cinaed had said. "Does anybody other than Blurr know that I run the Agency? Cinaed said John ran countries and the team. That doesn't mean she knows he directly runs the Agency. She would have warned me, or said something about it."

She tapped her lip. It felt odd with Paragon's thicker finger. "Do the agents know the Paragon is their boss? Well, they know he's *a* boss, but they don't act like he's *the* boss. Well, maybe some do, and some don't? That's a possibility. I need to figure that out. 33 and 34 might know, or be able to find out, if I'm careful. Crap. This stuff is complicated. But at least now I have a lead. I need to figure out how John's orders are coming in, and maybe I can trace them back to him. Or maybe the Agency runs itself and I'm chasing my flying tail."

She stared at her empty coffee cup and sighed. "Well, time to find out how much clout I have and declare it time to go home. But *after* I fix the spill wall. That needs to be done to prevent more flooding. This rain is not letting up."

Liza slid the pen into the clipboard, studied the terrain map, and then flew outside to finish the day's work. "I'm tired of being wet. I want my fuzzy nightgown. Heh. That would make an amusing photo op. Paragon prancing about in my tiny robe."

A few thousand sand bags later, she'd built up an improvised levee. After a few more tons of debris were cleared, they were flying back home. Liza discovered that the Blurr did sleep as he snored away on the plane, barely covered by a disposable blanket the stewardess gave him. He didn't toss, turn, or move while he slept, and he didn't look anything like Antonio Banderas. He looked to be about seventy, horribly malnourished and gaunt thin to the point where she could count every bone as it poked out of his skin. She tried not to stare at him, but did anyway, and she eventually decided he wasn't old but that his skin was heavily weathered, like a surfers. He woke briefly and consumed a dozen or more protein shakes before instantly falling back to sleep. "That's a high price for powers, but not as bad as Cinaed's. I wonder if Shokkusan has a downside. Cyber gave up being human. John hates being the Paragon. It's not fair. These people give their lives for us, and they have to suffer while doing it."

Liza was restless, so she tried to finish a Leon Ramiro novel that she'd been glancing at during the mission. The novel was interesting, but every time she picked up her bookmark she'd forgotten where she was in the story. She'd back up a few pages and try again, never moving the mark very far before putting the book down, and falling asleep with it in her lap.

Eventually, they were back in New York. She was half asleep on the long elevator ride to Paragon's apartment, her head resting on the humming wall.

Upon reaching the hall, she decided to go see Cinaed before turning in. Bleary eyed, she knocked on Cinaed's door only to have it opened by CyberSoldier.

"What the hell do you want?"

11

"Sorry," said Liza. "I just wanted to talk to Cinaed. Not important. It can wait for morning." Liza yawned.

"That's it? You haven't said a word to me in over a week, and you don't want anything? I don't get that."

Liza squinted as she tried and failed to make out what Cyber was implying from his body language. Half of his face, torso, and the left side of his body was unreadable cybernetic stuff. However, the rest of him wasn't covered in his usual armor, which allowed her to see that his exposed whiter-than-white skin looked pallid and dull, contrasting with the gleaming metal. He was wearing a deep red Kimono-like bathrobe, and it was a good color on him. She also noticed that it hung open too much in the front, enough that Liza had to keep her eyes on his face lest she catch more than the a casual glimpse of his manhood. The effort to not look, however, made her want to look more, mainly out of curiosity. Now that she had the same equipment, she was infinitely curious about how other men dealt with the extra appendage, especially in the type of tight pants the Paragon wore. Or how men did not make a mess while standing up to do their business? She was sure there was a trick to it, because she was getting it wrong every time. Half asleep as she pondered such random thoughts, she realized she was staring where she shouldn't.

"Hello? I said what is going on with you?" Cyber was yelling, but that seemed to be his normal conversational tone. As far as Liza could recall, Cyber always sounded like he was yelling.

"Nothing's wrong. I'm just tired. Why?" A thought kept rolling around in the back of her head that she'd had this conversation before, a déjà vu kind of feeling.

"Why? I want to know if you're gonna honor our deal, or is this gonna get real ugly, real quick?"

"Oh great," Liza thought, "I've found another of John's little fuck-with-people games."

Out loud she said, "Depends. Did you hold up your end of the bargain?"

Cyber jabbed a finger in Liza's face and moved in close enough to get his hot spittle all over her face as he managed to yell even louder. "For real? I've had it with you. It's now way past time you and me got dirty. One of us ain't gettin' back up!"

"Cyber," Liza started to say when his metal fist slammed into her jaw like a jackhammer. The pain was enough to make her see bright fairy lights, and she distantly felt the back of her head slam into the far wall. She tried clutching her jaw, but the pain wouldn't stop. Then a punch came in under her ribcage that crushed the wind out of her, lifted her off the ground, and smacked her head into the ceiling.

"It's *over*. I am out. You here me? *Out!*" His artificial foot slammed up between Liza's legs and hit her groin like a truck hitting a wall. The pain was sharp and horrific, but she couldn't cry out more than a whimper without air in her lungs. She tried breathing, but it hurt to breathe. She clutched her groin as she flopped onto the ground, but it did nothing to stop the searing pain.

"What's the matter with you?" Cinaed yelled as she came up from the living room, wrapping her nightgown about herself.

Liza didn't hear her or see her. She couldn't focus on anything but the pain. Everything hurt like needles shooting up under her skin. Hurt more than she'd ever been hurt. This was worse than the bullets.

Cinaed shoved Cyber, but he didn't budge. "I'll melt you to scrap if you don't get the hell away from him!"

"You'd defend that prick?" Cyber yelled back. "After all we've been through? After all he's done?"

Liza remained curled in a ball on the floor, clutching herself, praying for the pain to end.

"All we've been through is right. No one else could put up with a pigheaded jack ass like you!"

"You want me to make this about you, too? 'Cause I will, woman."

"Woman? I'm more of a man than you are half the time!"

"You did *not* go there."

"Hell yeah, I did! Going to cry about it?" Cinaed made a noise that sounded like a guinea pig eyeing fresh lettuce.

"That's cold, baby. Know what else is cold?" Cyber said, his voice shaky.

"Oh oh oh *stop it! Stop it!* Your hands are *freezing!*"

Liza forced herself to look up to see what was going on. Cyber had his hands under Cinaed's nightshirt. He didn't look like he was hurting her, more like…flirting?

Liza made herself sit up. Breathing still hurt, and she kept her legs wide apart, but everything else was a distant ache. "That's enough, Cinaed. It's ok. I had it coming. I deserved it."

"Damn right, you did. And we're not done," said Cyber, not sounding as fierce as he seemed to want to be.

"We're going to talk this out. Cyber and me. Man to man. You stay out of it, Cinaed," said Liza as she climbed to her feet, trying, and failing, to sound tough.

Cinaed glared daggers at her, so Liza added, "Please?"

"Fine. Be idiots. Pee all over the place and beat your chests." She shoved Cyber into the hall and closed the door. "*Men!*" could be heard from the other side of the door.

Cyber spat as he talked. "Also? I'm leaving. I'm done with this."

"Because of me and Cinaed?"

"No, moron. You know why."

"I don't. Humor me. It's been a long week."

"That's the way you want it? Fine." He jabbed his metal finger at Liza repeatedly as he growled. "I'm tired of this damned closet you keep me in. I don't give a damn about *your* image. I'm tired of pretending about mine. I don't care if they discharge me, and I'm tired of you threatening to discharge me. The world can survive having a gay hero. And if they can't? Fuck them. Fuck. Them. All. I don't care what small minds think. My people are people, too, and I'm not hiding it anymore."

Cyber shoved Liza hard enough to throw her to the ground. "Not hiding it for *you*. Not for *anyone*. *No more!*"

Liza's exhaustion vanished as she felt the adrenalin and testosterone kick in. She instantly got a second wind. She'd felt the same experience several times during the rescue mission, and she loved the feeling of that crazy high propelling her forward after she thought she had nothing left. She jumped to her feet, and Cyber took up a stance to knock her back down.

She wagged her finger 'no' at him. "First. You *know* I can take you. Won't be a problem. Second. I don't care if you're gay. Go tell the world. You've proven yourself a thousand times over. And you didn't even need to prove yourself because there is nothing wrong with you."

Liza leaned in and got right in his face. "You want to leave? Go. I won't stop you. But don't blame me. I want you here."

CyberSoldier blinked. He was speechless.

Liza smiled. She'd figured out the tough guy talk.

"You mean that? This ain't some new head game you're pulling?"

"I mean it. I've done a lot of thinking since I nearly died last week - and there are things I want to change. This is one of them."

Cyber looked him up and down. "For real? Shokkusan said you were acting all weird. Huh. Don't that beat all. You? Accepting me?"

Liza felt her stomach tighten. She'd gone too far. She needed to sound like a reformed John, but still be John, so she added, "Accepting? No. But as long as you stay on your side of the locker room, I'm fine."

CyberSoldier leaned back and stared for a bit, then shook it off. "Alright. Alright."

Cyber opened the door to his apartment and walked in, leaving the door open for Liza to follow him in, which she did. He paused at a metal table, opened a file drawer, took out a manila folder and handed it to Liza.

"That's the Intel on North Korea you wanted. Fools think I can't read lips or speak their dialect. You were right. They got a mess of centrifuges spittin' out fissionable material. Needs to be shut down, sovereign nation be damned. Ought to go out and deal with India and Pakistan too if you ask me."

"We don't go after the real bad guys, do we?" Asked Liza with genuine curiosity.

"You sound like you're having more than a change of heart. More like you replaced the whole damn thing."

"You could say that. Now could I have that talk with Cinaed?"

"You can talk, but I want this to end. I hate the tabloids making me sound all cuckolded."

"Cuckolded?"

"I don't know a better word. You want her, you have her. None of this sham marriage you two talked me into. I'm tired of looking like a man who can't control his own wife. It's humiliating."

"I made you do that," repeated Liza, finding she liked John even less then before. "Yes, I did. And you're right. No more. You two want to break up, break up. Has no impact on you being on the team. But you don't have to worry about her and me, um, doing it, anymore. We're done. With that. No more. No."

"What? Did I kick you too hard? Broke your dick?"

"No. We were done, already. Cinaed and I are friends, but that's all."

Cyber just stared as Liza knocked on the bedroom door and Cinaed let him in. "Huh. Straight folk are weird."

Liza didn't get the conversation she wanted. Cinaed was already three sheets to the wind on wine, and Cyber kept going in and out to make his opinion about anything and everything be known, and to make sure the two weren't doing anything they shouldn't be. Complicating matters more, Liza wanted to keep her secret identity known only to Cinaed and Shokkusan, so Cyber's presence ruined any chance of a real conversation. Eventually, Liza just gave up and went to Paragon's apartment.

On entering it, she knew something was wrong.

Things were tossed about, the place was ransacked. The more she looked, the more she saw. Couch cushions were pulled up and left on the ground. Drawers in the kitchen were opened. Liza turned and found the two safes were both wide open and empty.

"Damn it! He's been here!"

She looked about the bedroom and bath and found the same disarray. If not for the security door being secure, she'd assume she was robbed. It was John.

"Control!" she yelled into her suit mic. "There's been an intruder in my apartment. I want to know who, when, and how!"

She got a little thrill out of barking out orders. No one had ever listened to her before she was Paragon. She belatedly thought she sounded like her mother, which was not a kind thought, but it didn't dispel the thrill.

"Hold on, Colonel," said an impossibly awake and alert Control.

"What does he do?" she wondered to herself, "take caffeine from an I.V. drip?"

"Access check complete, Colonel. Um…All the entry and exit codes are yours, John."

"I was ass deep in sewage water and mosquitoes for five and a half days. Want to tell me how I pulled that off?"

"Oh. You're right. I didn't think about that. Damn. This is serious. I'll have agents there in less than a minute."

"Don't bother. My safe is empty. And I know who did it. That Liza girl you were supposed to be tracking down for me. How's that going, by the way?"

"Sir, I don't see how some hayseed from -"

Liza cut Control off in mid-sentence. "Somehow, she pulled this off. I don't let people in here, now I did, and I'm robbed. It's not a coincidence."

"You're right, sir. Of course, sir. We'll find her, sir."

"So you still haven't found her?"

"No, sir. She's fallen off the grid. Completely vanished. Closed all of her bank accounts, too."

"Weren't you watching her credit cards? Wouldn't closing her account have set off some kind of bells or something?"

"It's my mistake, sir. I wasn't considering the matter a high enough priority issue, and she wasn't rated as a credible threat after debriefing. Though looking back at her suspected association with Dr. Psi, her victim state could have been a ruse to throw us off our guard and invite her into our circle of trust. A pure Trojan horse attack."

"Let's go with that Trojan thing. Make this an issue. Big red alarm bell thing. Find her. Then tell me where she is so I can deal with her in person."

"Absolutely, Colonel. First priority. Working on it now."

"Good. I'm going to bed. Wake me when you know something or if my codes are used to enter or leave any place in this building."

"Colonel?"

"Yes?"

"What was in the safe? If you don't mind me asking. It may help with the investigation if I know what she took."

"I do mind you asking. Good night." Liza turned off the suit's microphone and braced herself against the edge of the couch with an unsteady hand. She was getting better at lying and acting, but it still scared the hell out of her.

She moved furniture to barricade the door and paced until the adrenalin wore off. She crawled into bed, sure she wouldn't be able to sleep, but she was out as soon as her head hit the pillow.

The morning brought a new mission, and an ugly one. The whole team was awake and assembled in the war room by seven AM, though none of them seemed to be really awake. Cinaed was clearly hung-over, and Shokkusan was dozing off. Blurr was almost sitting still, his chair barely vibrating. Cyber bucked the trend by being alert, attentive, and for him, chipper. His cybernetic body didn't need sleep, and the nano-machines in his blood that fought off infection also broke down the toxins in his body while producing their own artificial amphetamines. He had his own internal espresso machine, though Liza suspected their talk last night had also impacted his mood. Liza had learned that trivia from Cinaed, and now, as she sipped her own coffee, wondered if something similar was percolating within Control.

The briefing was given by Agent 17, the expert in the Indian/Pakistani conflict, though an expert was hardly needed to understand the problem or the implications. Radicals from Pakistan, armed with explosives, had broken into and taken over both the Indian and Pakistani parliaments in a coordinated terrorist attack. They were making some kind of demand about Kashmir, but no one cared. The only thing both countries wanted was the men dealt with quickly, before war broke out. Each country kept tens of thousands of troops on each other's borders, and both had nuclear weapons. A war could happen instantly and end just as quickly in a radioactive cloud. So far, the rival countries had worked together against the common terrorist enemy, but the nationality of the enemy was clear, as many of them openly wore the uniforms of the Pakistani military. No amount of disavowing was going to stop the bloodshed once the name calling began in earnest.

Within the hour they were wheels up. Throughout the flight they were briefed over and over. Video screens with heads of state chimed in, and agents brought in experts from several intelligence agencies from multiple countries. They were all men, and they looked to Paragon for direction and reassurance. Liza faked it for a while, but the pleading and the whining became too much. She even told the NATO commander to grow a pair before hanging up on him.

As they passed over Europe, Liza started shooting from her hip because no one else was. "CyberSoldier and Blurr will take the Pakistani capital, New Dehli, the rest of us will go to Islamabad in India. We'll hit both at the same time." There was much debate and plotting and planning that followed once a course of action was set, like a chain of dominoes that needed the initial push. Liza couldn't keep up with it all. She had no idea if her idea was any good, but apparently any idea was better than no idea at all.

Secretly, she also had a hunch that both Blurr and CyberSoldier were looking for a chance to show off and cement their new relationships with Paragon. They would be fine.

It was the girl team that Liza was worried about. They had lots of firepower, but this was not the kind of place to use it; too many innocents could be harmed. Untold numbers of civilians and diplomats were being held hostage by terrorists loaded with guns and suicide-ready bombers. It was the worst kind of conflict because the bad guys wanted bad things to happen to everyone and cared little what happened to them.

There was a second reason she worried about the girls. Liza had never killed anyone, or let anyone die. Every time she thought about this operation, she was convinced she wouldn't get out of it without a lot of people getting hurt. She'd seen her first dead bodies during her first rescue operations, and she saw them again and again when she slept, but she wasn't a part of their deaths. Liza didn't think she could do what needed to be done, and there was no way out of it. Cinaed and Shokkusan kept stealing glances her way, but they kept silent.

Four hours after they landed, it was over.

Liza flew Cinaed onto the top of the building, and she flooded the ventilation system with waves of extreme heat. It turned out that it doesn't take much to overheat someone when it's already a hundred degrees out. Meanwhile, Liza flew Shokkusan around as a living Taser gun, zapping anyone they could find into drooling incapacity. At one point, Liza was directed to an inner room where some hostages were held, and she had to punch through the walls to get there. Punching stone hurt, but the adrenalin and the horror of it all drove the pain from her attention. Shokkusan followed and arced out a webbed curtain of power that zapped everyone in the room, friend or foe.

Liza started to think, she had been wrong, that they would get through this without anyone being hurt. Then a suicide bomber charged her from behind, grabbed her around the waist and exploded the C4 strapped to his body. Liza was blown out the hole she had made in the building and smacked into a metal barricade erected outside. She couldn't hear anything for a few moments other than a loud, ringing buzz. She looked at herself and saw portions of her clothing shredded away and every part of her covered in gore.

She screamed.

She found herself flying without ever thinking about flying. She was traveling at a speed capable of making sonic booms in the air, and the wind ripped off more of her clothing and some of the mess, but not enough. She saw a large body of water and plunged into it. The force of the impact upon the water sent spray hundreds of feet into the air and drove out surf-quality waves. The impact knocked her unconscious and she plunged into the briny depths. Paragon's body was heavy, and it sank.

She woke up on the silty bottom, unconscious until the cold water woke her. She couldn't see in the murky dark, and she panicked at not being able to breathe. She struggled and thrashed at imaginary choking feelings that her mind told her she should be having, but her body checked in and said it was fine. She didn't need to breathe. That, or the Paragon body could hold its breath for a very long time.

Eventually she calmed down enough from the false sensation of drowning to recall what had brought her here, and she began vigorously scrubbing herself clean with sand and grit. She scrubbed until it hurt, and then scrubbed some more. Then she rocketed out of the water into the air with a single thought. She spun in the air whipping the water off of her. She screamed again and again until there was no will left to scream. Spent, she sobbed a bit as she hung in the air and tried to figure out where she was.

She landed on the shore, and the Indian fishermen that had been watching her scattered like roaches in the light. She soared back into the sky when she saw the disturbing image of fear on their faces. She continued to fly until she saw a city. It didn't take long to find one, and when she did it was dwarfed by the never-ending shantytowns that surrounded it.

She checked and found that her com was destroyed, most of it gone, the rest charred and waterlogged. She didn't know what to do. The world was huge.

She wandered in the sky for an hour, hugging herself, and shivering. She saw some planes and followed them until she found an airport, a tiny cross in a tangle of buildings. She landed on the tower that watched the runway. There was a door on the roof, which she opened with a yank hard enough to shatter the lock that held it closed. She glided down the short stairwell and was greeted by shouting people. Some of them had drawn guns or made improvised weapons out of whatever was handy. "I need clothes," said Liza, "Then call the Defense Force." There was a cacophony of responses, none of them English. Liza found a chair and sat down and repeated herself. Lots of arms waved in the chaos, but she caught a mix of heavily accented English in the mess. She stamped her foot on the ground with enough force to put her foot through it. The room shook and few people were knocked to the floor. Everyone went silent, and she repeated herself. Quickly, a blanket appeared and was handed to her. She wrapped it about herself. Security people and soldiers arrived, and there was even more commotion, but no one came near her. Eventually, they asked nicely if she could come downstairs so that the men could go back to doing their job of guiding planes. Liza nodded and followed them. She didn't walk; she floated.

She was brought to a mostly white room and had many people speaking to her in pleasant soft tones of melodic pseudo-English. They offered her food and drink and anything she wanted while she waited. Medical experts offered to examine her. Liza huddled in the blanket and ignored them all until they brought her a phone. "Colonel?" Control was on the other end.

"I don't know where I am," said Liza. "The bomb…" She stopped talking for a long minute as flashbacks swarmed her senses. "The bomb," she whispered, "messed me up."

"We have agents on route, sir. You're safe where you are. Don't worry. We've got this."

Liza hung up without a reply and shivered under the blanket until her team arrived to take her home.

An hour later, she was back in the air on a Defense Force plane. In addition to the Agents in black, and the fancy costumes the powers wore, the Defense Force had field agents in jumpsuits that did most of the menial work. She was wearing one of these 'DF' suits. She was alone on the flight, except for a couple of Agents who kept to themselves. They did take the time to debrief her and let her know that the Agency was handling the press before getting up and moving to the other side of a curtained partition.

When Liza heard about the bloodbath in Pakistan, she got sick inside. Combined, Blurr and Cyber had killed nearly a hundred hostile forces. Only two civilians were injured. None of the terrorists walked away. At the Indian Parliament only few people died, but there were hundreds of injuries, many severe.

According to UNSAD Agent 63, this was a successful mission given the low number of civilian casualties. Liza just stared at him as if he were insane.

Liza excused herself and went into the too small bathroom and stayed there for the rest of the flight. She cried a few times, and got sick once, but by the time they landed, she was able to compose herself enough to come out with a stoic face. She ignored everyone and went up to her apartment. Since the old Paragon seemed to treat people the same way, no one found her behavior odd.

She locked the door behind her when she reached her room, peeled off her uniform, and went straight into the shower. She turned the water on as hot and as hard as it could go. She wanted to feel something, and as the water burned down on her, she sank to her knees and curled up in the corner. When she closed her eyes, she heard screaming and explosions and the images of the massacre in Pakistan and saw red blood everywhere.

She was done being a hero. She wanted to go home.

She left the shower and put on a clean Paragon suit, turned off the suit com, went up the staircase to the roof, and flew out.

At first, she had no idea where she was going, or even where she was in the city. New York was confusing to her, and flying above it didn't improve anything.

She decided to see how fast she could fly. She picked a direction away from the water and flew off with a sonic boom that left her ears ringing. She went up high, bursting through the cloud layers, and was nearly blinded by how brilliant the sun was. She wasn't sure how high she could safely fly, but already the air was too thin to breathe, so she went back down to just below the clouds. She flew as fast as she could and gained a new understanding of just how huge the world was, and how small she was. She could feel the wind thrashing at her and knew she was moving fast, but the world still rolled by slowly beneath her. She slowed down when she recognized the bulges of the Great Lakes, especially Erie. She'd done a project in elementary school on the lakes using modeling clay and remembered the shapes well.

From this height, cities seemed to all blur together into one never-ending metropolitan area, interspersed with a surprising amount of green, but she figured out which one Cleveland was and followed the ribbon of I-71 south. When she reached Columbus, she was less sure of the way and flew lower until she was only a few hundred feet above the roads. From this height she could find her way home.

As she flew by towns she knew, she wondered why she hadn't done this before. The constant recognition of the things she knew, seen in different ways, the discovery of sites she'd never seen so close to home...it was amazing, the most fun she'd had since becoming Paragon. She spiraled in the air for the sheer joy of flight. She tried tricks like loops and combination barrel rolls going one way then the other. She tried flying backwards and upside down. She flew with her head to the ground and her feet to the clouds. She flew arms and legs out and flapping like a snow angel, and then all tucked in like a cannonball. As she flew lower, though, bugs became a problem. They felt like pinches in random spots because she was flying so fast, and when she realized what they were, and the mess they made, she was grossed out and flew up higher into the air.

She disturbed flocks of birds, and they flowed from a telephone wire to a tree like a blanket fluttering down. So Liza flew with them, and they dispersed into two panicked clouds going left and then right. She followed one and was amazed at how quickly they could change direction. When the flock flew forward, she tried a full reverse, flying back where they came from, and, to her surprise, a few birds followed, then the whole amorphous mass followed. She led them back and forth and then landed on a power line she'd seen a few other birds sitting on. She wasn't sure if she'd get shocked, or if she'd break the line sitting on it, so she hovered over it by an inch. The birds seem to be able to land unharmed, and they chattered out in a deafeningly loud discussion.

It was the first time she could recall having *fun* as the Paragon, and she wanted to share it with someone. She wanted to share it with Gwen.

She tore off for home in a gust that sucked all the birds back into the air in her wake. They eventually recovered, amid loud complaints, a few tried to follow Liza, but she was long gone.

Slowly, she began weaving as she flew, and her visual focus became a blurry strain. She landed in a soybean field and staggered into a jogging, stumbling, half-run of a stop before collapsing to her knees. She found she was beyond exhaustion, and fell back on the plants. Liza stared up at the clouds overhead as they moved slowly past and thought of dashing through the foggy vapor and seeing the bright sun emerge. She closed her eyes as she imagined the flight and fell asleep for what she told herself was a brief cat nap that turned into an eight hour slumber in the field.

She woke to the sound of helicopters and the wind and dirt kicked up by their landing. Cinaed got out, along with several agents, but they let her go forward first. Liza sat up bleary eyed, and wiped the sleep sand from her eyes, and then choked a bit on the dust being kicked up. Cinaed went right up to Liza, knelt down beside her, and spoke right into her ear to be heard over the roar of the helicopters and so that no one else could hear.

"You had us worried."

"How did you find me?"

"Your suit, dummy. Even turned off, the com is connected and can be tracked. Next time you run away, take off the suit."

"I just couldn't take it," Liza said. "We killed those men."

Cinaed gave Liza a short hug, then got up and walked over to the waiting agents and talked to them. Some nodded; then they climbed back into the black copters and flew off. Cinaed walked back like she was carrying a heavy weight on her shoulders.

"You're welcome," she said, sitting back down, and then she gave Liza a real hug.

Liza didn't let go for a time, and she had to wipe her eyes when she did. "What did you tell them?" she asked.

"A lie. And I called in a few favors." Cinaed brushed Liza's tangled hair into place gently with her hands. "How old are you?"

"I'm not a kid."

"I know that. I'm twenty-five and I've been in the game since I was sixteen. Before that, I was really messed up. With my power, any strong emotion means fire. I hurt a lot of people. Most by accident, but some on purpose. I've been a ward of the state since I was born, but no one survives around me unscarred. This hero life is the only thing I have that turns my destruction into something good. I don't have a clue how many people have died because of me, or how many I've saved."

"Wow," said Liza, brushing away her own tears as Cinaed held her. "I'm sorry. That's… That's horrible."

"Yeah. Wasn't a Norman Rockwell life."

Liza suddenly leaned away from the embrace. "No offense, but just because you had it genuinely awful doesn't change anything. That was your life, this is mine. I'm responsible for what I did."

Cinaed was taken aback. She was used to pity and courted it at times. "My point was that…Fuck. I don't know what my point was."

Liza stared back at Cinaed. "Does it get any easier?" She stared until Cinaed looked away. "It doesn't, does it?"

"Not really. You just sort of turn parts of yourself off so you can go on and do what you have to do." Cinaed stood up and brushed herself off. "Then you run into someone new to all of this, someone like you, and it's like those parts turn back on all by themselves and you have to relearn to turn them back off. That never gets easy. At all."

Liza got to her own feet. "I want my life back. It wasn't anything great, but it was mine. People weren't dying around me. I wasn't crying myself to sleep over people I couldn't save! A bad day for me is freezing because I can't afford the gas bill. That's pretty awesome compared to drowning or being blown up by someone who hates you enough they're willing to kill themselves."

"That's where you were running to, wasn't it? Home?"

"Yeah. Almost got there, too. But I have no idea what I would have done when I got there. No one would recognize me." Liza's fists clenched. "Guess I was hoping to find that asshole, John, sitting on my couch in my flannel ducky pajamas, eating my peanut butter. Don't know what I'd do then. But he knows how to fix this. I know he does."

"He's probably not there," Cinaed said as she wiped her own eyes. "If he's hiding from us, then he won't go anywhere we'd expect."

Liza crossed her arms. "Why did you come out here?"

"Because Paragon is a jackass and you're not. I need a better reason than that?"

"I guess not. I used to think you were a jackass. I'm glad I was wrong."

"You weren't wrong. I am a jackass. And I've got my own condo in hell reserved just for me. Don't ever forget it. I've a lot to atone for. Being nice to you isn't going to buy me any tickets to heaven or snowballs in hell."

"So now what?" Liza looked around and saw a tractor in the distance. "Your ride left."

"They're a phone call away. But you're my ride, for now. Let's go check out your house and figure things out from there. I'm a better liar than you, and I know John better than you. You need me."

Liza's crossed arms turned into a self-hug and a shiver.

Cinaed held out her hand. "I bought us a day or two before the agents come back on their own, so let's go."

Liza took the hand and pulled her close, and they hugged once more. Neither said anything as they both quietly put their mental armor back on. Liza broke the embrace, nodded, and said, "Ok. But this is my life. My lead."

Cinaed nodded. "Agreed."

12

Liza had never flown anyone for more than a mile. From the rescue mission in the Cayman's, she'd learned that it was not easy to carry people around. Arms don't support a body's weight very well. Most people suffer bruising or pain, and there's no easy way to yank someone into the air from the mid section. She'd experimented by making a chair out of her arms, but most people didn't fit, and they wriggled. She'd tried using an actual chair, but chairs turned out to be easily broken when carrying passenger weight. When she couldn't find a chair, she had tried to piggyback her passenger, but people would panic and cover their faces with their hands, or they weren't strong enough to hang on. The best method she'd discovered was to wrap them in her arms and legs like an intimate spooning embrace, it was creepy, but it allowed Liza to keep a good grip and to shield the passenger with her body. Cinaed refused. So Liza tried carrying her like a child, swaddled in her arms. It worked, but Cinaed's hair whipped about in her face. Liza did her best to ignore it.

Liza kept her altitude as she flew to just a few hundred feet above the road so she could follow it and not get lost.

Flying that low also meant that there were many chances to be seen. Cars pulled off the road; people got out to look or leaned out of windows; dogs barked in front yards and in the back of pickup trucks, and drivers honked their horns. As they approached a small town, a few people were out on their porches, and all of them got out of their chairs to lean out over the rail to watch. A few called out. When they reached the outer limits of Clarksdale, a police car began following them, lights flashing and siren blaring. Liza, ignoring the commotion she caused, kept flying.

Liza found her apartment, and when she landed outside, the police car pulled over and the Sheriff got out, hand resting on his holster, the other touching his cap like a cautious salute. "Evenin' folks."

Liza set Cinaed down gently and noticed that the Sheriff couldn't take his eyes off of her. Her skintight black suit with red flames up the sides was tight enough to be painted on, and her body was tighter and perkier than it needed to be. Cinaed drank like a fish, but she still worked out.

Liza cleared her throat. "Officer. Can we help you?"

"Was about to ask you something right similar. Not every day we get flying people come visit us. What brings your kind to my little town?"

Cinaed gave him her best glare. "Your town? Is there some kind of problem, officer," she read his badge, "Brown?"

"It's Sheriff Brown, and that depends on you. This is a quiet town. We don't take kindly to public disturbances."

Cinaed started to say something, but Liza put her hands on her shoulders and turned her towards the apartment. "Sounds good, because we don't want any disturbances either. Just seeing a friend, and then we'll be on our way."

"I'll just wait out here to be sure."

The heroes marched up the walk without looking back. Cinaed added as they reached the door, "Just let me heat up his belt buckle. Just warm his junk up enough to make him yelp."

"Maybe later." Liza pressed the buzzer for her own apartment.

Cinaed started humming, "Chestnuts roasting on an open fire." Liza hushed her.

"Hello?" squawked Gwen's voice over the tinny and ancient intercom. "Who is it?"

"It's me – I mean a friend of Liza's," said Liza, "I'm the Paragon."

"Smooth," Cinaed muttered.

"*Oh my goodness!*" Gwen squealed in a vocal range best heard only by dogs. "Oh. But she's not here!"

Liza looked at Cinaed, her frustration clear on Paragon's face. "Was she here? I mean recently?"

"Sure. But she left. You wouldn't know where she is, would you?"

"Two - I mean ma'am - could we talk to you about this? In person? Can we come up?"

"Okay!" The door buzzed and Liza opened it and went in. The door swung closed on CinaedCinaed. She caught it just before it latched. Liza was halfway up the stairs and moving a bit faster than human normal.

"If you're pretending to be a boy, you could at least open doors for the penile-challenged," Cinaed growled as she followed Liza up the steps to the second floor.

"If you're going to be an adult," growled Liza as she paused for Cinaed to catch up, "you could at least stop dressing like a pre-teen ice skater."

"Heh. I like you better when you fight back," said Cinaed while she gestured at Liza's pants.

Liza's bottom suddenly got painfully hot and she jumped and smacked it. "*Ow!*"

169

She was turning to yell at Cinaed when the door to the apartment opened. Gwen was standing there rocking back and forth on her toes, clutching a mug of tea, and wearing oversized pink flannel pajamas with non-matching blue bunny slippers.

Liza ground her teeth instead of yelling at Cinaed, and held out her hand to Gwen. "Hello. I'm the Paragon."

Gwen looked at the Paragon wide-eyed. She gripped her mug without budging. "You are!"

Cinaed put her hand on Liza's shoulder. "He is. And I'm *the Kennaye*."

Gwen stared at them both.

"Can we come in?" Cinaed asked.

"Okay," said Gwen as she backed up with a shuffling motion to push the door open. Then, instead of getting out of the way, she made herself thin so they could squeeze past.

Liza strode into the living room and looked around before drifting about and touching things lightly. It seemed a decade had passed since she was last here. Even still, she could tell the changes. "He was here."

Cinaed remained at the edge of the room looking disapprovingly at the lack of cleanliness and the lack of wealth. "She. You mean *she* was here."

Liza's voice sounded like she was a million miles away when she answered, "Yeah… She."

Gwen swung the door shut a bit too loudly. Cinaed jumped. Liza just smiled, used to it. Gwen crossed over to the kitchenette. "Can I get you anything? I have water. And tea. Several kinds of tea. Green teas. Herbal teas. No black teas, though. They frighten me."

Cinaed raised an eyebrow. "Frighten you?"

"It's the black leaves," said Liza, still in a nostalgic daze. "They look like ashes, and they remind her of when she burned her diaries. Don't ask. It's a long story."

"It is," agreed Gwenifer Two Tales. "How did you know?"

"Liza told me," said Liza with a solemn tone. "She told me a lot about you."

"She didn't tell me anything about you. Except that you're a wonderful kisser, and that you fill out a bathrobe nicely. Oh wait. I shouldn't have said that part. It's clear you do," she said while staring unabashedly at Paragon's crotch, "but it's not the sort of thing you should say to guests. I'm pretty sure it's not."

Cinaed covered her mouth so as not to laugh. "I'll say it to a guest, so you go right ahead, darling."

Liza flushed. Then she quickly cleared a pile of laundry off the couch and sat down. "Water please."

"I'm good," said Cinaed as she moved to sit on the edge of the couch next to Liza.

Gwen disappeared into the tiny kitchen off the entrance hall. She reappeared with a bottle of water and handed it to Liza. "I saw you on the news. You look shorter. How come you're not out catching bad guys?"

Liza couldn't help but smile. Hearing Gwen's voice had that affect on her.

Cinaed jumped in, "Actually, miss, that's why we're here. Some bad men are after Elisabeth, and we need to find her to protect her."

Liza nodded in agreement.

"Wow," said Gwen. "She has the weirdest boy troubles."

"It's not boy troubles," snapped Liza.

"She's not here, though," said Gwen. "Does that mean she's in trouble now? Could she be locked up somewhere pleading for her life while we sit here drinking tea?"

"I doubt it," said Cinaed. "What did she do or say when she was here, and where did she go? Where might she have gone?"

"Wow. That's deep. That's a lot to ponder, too." Gwen stared up at the ceiling, "Where do you want me to start?"

Liza watched Gwen draw in a breath. She had an audience asking her questions, and she was going to let it all out. Liza let her. "Let's start from the beginning. When did you first see her?"

"Well, it was first grade, and I was trying to sell lemonade by crushing up Sweet Tart candies in water, and Liza gave me a nickel and choked on it and said it was horrible and wanted her money back. I wouldn't give it back because she drank it already, so she got mad and pulled my pony tail, which my mom had just put up when I asked her to because I'd seen this movie and the girl in the movie had to find her stray dog and she had a pony tail, and the dog looked like my dog, which wasn't my dog, it was my neighbor's dog, but I fed it so I considered it mine..."

Liza smiled. She missed her friend's rambling. Cinaed, on the other hand, stared blankly at Two Tales. "We meant, when did you *recently* see her?"

"Oh yeah. I could see that." Gwen looked sad for a moment, then brightened and launched into a new story.

Gwen told them everything in excruciating detail and needed prompting from time to time to skip ahead or to get back on track when she wandered off topic, especially when it came to mentioning Liza's new car. She kept finding ways to wax rhapsodic about the Jaguar John drove up in.

Cinaed wandered off at some point in frustration, ostensibly looking for tea, but she found Vodka instead and then got distracted finding something to mix with it and squealed when she found a can of V8.

Liza listened patiently to Gwen, mainly because she just wanted to hear her talk. It was the most normal she had felt since she woke up in the hospital. That warm nostalgia collapsed when Gwen meandered towards the end of her tale. "So Liza told me that she had to go away for awhile. At first she said it was a school project thing, but I didn't believe her. I was sure it was this guy she was talking to."

"Guy?" asked Liza. "You haven't mentioned a guy before."

"Well, I don't know for sure there was a guy. She would hide it. Only talk to him when I was out, that kind of thing. But she's never been good at hiding stuff, and I could tell something was up. And since she only gets that way around boys, I knew that was it. I even poked around her stuff a little, don't tell her, but even though I didn't find any proof, she must have figured out I was looking because she started getting moody and got real distant." There was hurt in Gwen's voice, and it tore at Liza. "But in the end she came around. Maybe a bit too much." Gwen sounded timid and uncertain and didn't continue.

"Came around how?" Liza finally prompted.

"Well, there was always a chemistry between us, you know? But I always knew she was too afraid to go *there*, and I was okay with that because life is more about living than sex, you know? So it's not something I was expecting to happen, like ever. But when she stepped into my shower, I just thought she was tired of waiting for me to get out and wanted some of the hot water before it ran out, but I should have known that wasn't the thing because she fixed the hot water tank! We always have hot water. Well, she put her arms around me all of a sudden, and I jumped like a mile because I wasn't expecting it and I'm ticklish there, but then I caught on and did my best to be supportive because you don't want to ruin someone's first time."

"*Stop!*" The arm on the couch snapped in Liza's grip. "Skip that part. What came next? *After* the shower?"

Cinaed was leaning against the entranceway, an eyebrow raised in amusement. Liza's face was pure blood rage.

"Ok. Well, it carried on for a day or so. Here and there," she said pointing about the room. "It was so not like her! But I figured it had been a while and she was really pent up, you know? Plus there's all that new experiment stuff to get out of the way, so I was okay with that even though I could have used some down time. But that's what friends are for, right?"

Cinaed watched Liza turn redder and redder. "Please, skip ahead to the part where she left."

"That was just it," said a clearly upset Gwen. "She just left! Out of nowhere, poof! Gone! We were getting along so well! I thought I did something wrong, you know? Or she couldn't handle what had happened. That happens sometimes. And we'd had an argument you know? We hadn't talked about what happened and I thought we should, but Liza just stormed out, said she had 'things'. I had no idea what she meant, but I wanted to be supportive, so I didn't argue. I took a nap and I was kinda stressed so I took some over the counter stuff and when I woke up she was gone. All of her old stuff was boxed up in her room, like it is now. All her new stuff, the stuff she'd bought, that was just gone. Even that cute coat she was gonna let me keep. Gone. The car? Gone. Not a word to me. Not even a note. I felt horrible, but her things were still boxed up so I thought she'd come back for them, at least. I thought it was something I'd said, that I'd pushed her too far, something. After a few days of waiting, I figured out she was gone for good, or something terrible had happened to her. I imagined all kinds of terrible things, and I watched the news, but there was nothing. I thought about calling the police, but she'd left on her own, and I tried to honor her choice. I didn't want to make things worse. I just didn't know what to do. It was hard."

Gwen's face had twisted up as she spoke, and by the end, she was openly sobbing.

Cinaed went over and gave her a brief hug and handed her a drink. Gwen knocked it straight back. Liza was on her feet and pacing, trying very hard not to make booming steps or break anything else, though she wanted nothing more than to smash everything she could get her hands on. Her hands clenched and unclenched.

"What's the matter with him?" asked Gwen. "Did I say something wrong? I'm always saying something wrong."

"No, dear," said Cinaed. "He's just worried about your friend. The departure sounds too abrupt. He's afraid that something might be wrong."

"I should have called the police! I knew it! Stupid!" Gwen started hitting her own head with the flat of her palm.

Cinaed grabbed her wrists and stopped her. "You didn't do anything wrong. Trust me."

Liza stopped pacing, "*Screw this*. I'm going to tell her."

Cinaed let go and waved her hands. "*No!* It's not going to help anything. It will only make things worse. Ignorance, in this case, *is* bliss."

Liza ground her teeth, while almost hyperventilating. "*But I. Can't. Live. With. What. He. Did!*"

"You know how you're feeling now? You want to *share* that feeling with your friend?"

"No," Liza said, deflating. She turned away. "I hate this."

Gwen watched the exchange and asked in a sobbing voice, "What am I missing?"

"It's just frustration, hon," said Cinaed. "Paragon is just more worried than he needs to be. He does that."

"Can you help her?" asked Gwen in a frail voice.

"Yes," said Liza. "I promise you."

"Oh, thank you," said Gwen as she slowly approached him. "You know she has a crush on you, right? Be careful with her. She's kind of fragile. And a little funny around people. But she's a great person. You guys would make a great couple! Just make the first move, though, because she's always too shy to try anything. Well, mostly." Gwen blushed and grinned.

"We're leaving." Liza stomped out of the room.

"We'll keep in touch," said Cinaed as she followed Liza out.

Before they even reached the walkway outside, Liza lifted Cinaed and flew off at the fastest pace she could with Cinaed in her arms. That turned out to be too fast, and Cinaed covered her eyes as her hair whipped Liza's face. The gust of their passing made the sheriff stagger and blew his hat far down the street.

"I need a helmet or something. How do you see?" screamed Cinaed over the roaring wind as they arced into the sky.

Liza slowed down slightly. "Dunno. I'm the Paragon. I just do."

Liza was silent as she flew over to the local big box store and landed. Cinaed shivered like she was entering a sewer as Liza hovered outside. A crowd quickly gathered to point up at her, but Liza ignored them. Cinaed came out with a black motorcycle helmet with a flaming skull on the side. Liza swooped down, picked her up, and rocketed off with a sonic boom that set off every car alarm in the parking lot.

Conversation at that speed, with that much wind, was impossible. It was also cold, and Cinaed had to use her powers not to freeze. Liza made a beeline back to New York without a word. She didn't slow down until she could recognize the island of Manhattan between the rivers. The trip took less than an hour.

"Guide me to HQ," Liza growled as she slowed from supersonic to car speeds.

"Just call Control," said Cinaed.

"I don't trust Control. I don't trust the Agency. John's Agent One, and he's still in charge."

"Then why the hell are we here?"

"I want to see Control in person."

"He knows where we are. The suits. Remember?"

"I know. I'm going to ditch that soon. I just don't want to have this conversation with him over the com. I want it face to face."

"So don't have the conversation. He can still talk you in."

"*Kinny!* Show me how to get there!"

"Don't be such a shit." She waved her arm. "Go that way more."

With Cinaed's help, Liza landed on the roof and set her down. The roof had a helipad, and agents were outside waiting for them. Liza stomped right past them into the building. The door was locked, but Liza just ripped it off its hinges and went in.

"Girl problems," Cinaed said to the stunned agents as she took off the helmet and tried to fix her hair before following Liza, in a full out run to catch up. "Slow down. Not all of us are super fast."

Liza came to a dead stop at the bottom of the stairs and punched the wall, putting her fist through a foot of steel-reinforced concrete.

Cinaed slowed down on the steps. "Liza?"

"He raped her," Liza said through clenched teeth.

"It…It wasn't rape. It was consensual. Nobody forced anybody."

Liza smashed the side of her fist into the adjacent wall with similar effect. Red lights and alarms went off everywhere. "If she knew the truth, it would *not* have happened! And he raped me! He used my life to do things…" She kicked an even larger hole and made the floor shake as she struck a support beam with a loud *klang*.

Cinaed talked into her com, "Stand down. Boss is just mad. For everyone's safety, stand down. I've got it under control."

"I'm going to *kill* him!" Liza yelled as Cinaed cut the mic.

"So kill him. Just stop smashing our home, or the suits will come and lock you away and you won't get to kill him."

"I'd like to see them try." Liza scowled.

"Liza, this is serious. You need to calm down."

"No. I need to act calm, but I am *not* calming down. *I can't forgive this.*"

"So don't. What's your plan? Do you actually have one?"

"I'm going to see if Control can be trusted. If he can, I'm going to tell him everything. He's been looking for me, when he should be looking for him. I'm betting, if he has all the details, he can try something he hasn't so far."

"And if not?"

"Then I'm fucked."

"Ok, no plan B. So let's make plan A work."

"You should get off here. Your ride's over," said Liza as she considered punching another hole.

"No deal. I'm sticking with you. I can't have you killing him. Smacked around, maybe, but not killed. I'm not going to let you fall that far."

"Good luck with that." Liza turned abruptly and stalked off towards the door to the stairs.

Liza stomped down the hall with jack hammer foot stomps, past Shokkusan who was in the hall waiting for them. Shokkusan stared as Cinaed took her aside. Liza went into Paragon's apartment. A few minutes later she emerged, wearing a plain white t-shirt, grey flannel pajama pants, and no shoes. She saw Cinaed talking to Shokkusan, so she walked up and interrupted them. "These clothes are clean of that tracking tech, right?"

Shokkusan gestured and a tingle of electricity rolled over Liza's body. "You're clean." Shokkusan looked to Cinaed, then to Liza, then back.

"You told her," said Liza. It was not a question.

"Yeah," said Cinaed. "Not all of it, but enough."

Liza looked down at Shokkusan, who only came up to Paragon's abs in height, and scowled, "Why?"

"We're a team for a reason," pleaded Cinaed. "We each have skills the other doesn't. You need us."

Shokkusan stared defiantly.

Liza muttered, "I can handle anything. I'm the Paragon, aren't I?"

"So was John," said Cinaed. "He knows everything about you, and he's the sneakiest bastard I know. You can't go after him alone. It won't end well."

There was an awkward pause, and then Liza, who had been lost in thought, looked up. "I'm going alone. This is my problem. Mine to fix. But there is something I want you to do. Tell the team. Tell them everything. They need to know in case something happens to me, or in case John comes back. They need to be ready for that. His days of controlling people are over." Her knuckles cracked as she flexed her fists.

"Alright," said Cinaed. "After we talk to Control."

"No. Now."

"So it's your turn to boss us around, is that it?"

"No. I'm just not wasting any more time. That bastard has been ahead of me from the beginning. Splitting up makes more sense to me. You know the guys, I don't. They'll believe you and listen to you. I'll talk to Control."

Liza didn't wait for a response. She stalked off to the elevator.

Minutes later, she was walking into the basement lab in which Control lived. This time, as she passed, she paid attention to all of the other worker bees buzzing about and conservatively estimated that Control had about thirty people working for him, and none of them would meet her gaze. Control emerged from his den of computers and met her in the common area, which consisted of a folding table in a break room covered in spare printer parts, cables, and stacks of discs.

"Sir? Are you ok?" Control asked as he came in and set down a clipboard. "We're estimating thirty to forty thousand dollars in building repairs, and we don't have the budget to do those kind of repairs in light of the congressional spending freezes."

"We need to talk in private. Find a secure place without listening devices, including your own. This is *Triple Top Secret.*"

"Triple Top Secret?"

"Don't argue. I made that up because this is really *really* secret. So just do it."

"I don't know if I can do that in this building, unless you want to —"

"No compromises. If that's what we need, dump your gear, we'll go outside. Now."

Several curious techs had managed to loiter within earshot, much like they had when Liza visited before. Liza stood up. "*Now!*" she barked, and Control jumped and then ran off into his lab. Breathing hard, he returned a moment later.

"All systems are set in standby and record mode, so I won't miss anything. I have to follow protocol. Also, while I'm on shift, my chip can't go off network for more than five minutes without sounding alarms, but I've activated firewalls and feedback loops to make it look like I'm still online. I can set our debriefing room down here to level three. We should be totally isolated from outside electronics, and the sound dampeners should be proof against physical surveillance."

"Big change from couldn't do it," said Liza with a death stare.

"I can't, not 100 percent, but I can block enough that only I have access. There isn't anything I can block 100 percent from myself."

"If I'm talking to you, why would I want to block that conversation from you? That doesn't make any sense."

"I'm required to log everything."

"Ah. You can't do that. Not this time."

"I'm under orders, sir. Maybe you should talk to someone else about whatever this is?"

"Why? You just told me I can't keep you out, so why not talk to you? You're the best."

"Thank you, sir, but what makes me the best is that I follow the protocols."

"Liar. You bend whatever rules you need to in order to do your job. And I think you know my true place in the Agency, don't you?"

Control looked about the room, noting the eavesdroppers. "I do, sir. You come first."

"Then follow my orders. Set up whatever tech voodoo you need so we can talk. Then you are under orders not to repeat it." Liza was so mad she didn't have to pretend to sound intimidating and authoritarian. She just was. "Got it?"

He nodded and led her down to the end of the hall and swiped an access card to get into a smallish room that had little more than a single round Formica table with three metal mesh chairs and an imposing steel file cabinet with the kind of combination locks you use on safes. The walls were coated in the kind of sound-proofing material used in recording studios. Once inside, Control locked the door and it hissed with a pneumatic seal. "We use this room to hold top secret documents and for meetings with the CIA and NSA. It should work for us." Control set a box on the table and flipped a toggle switch on it, which made a green light go on, and a barely audible hum filled the room. "This is a soundbox we assembled down here from spare parts. We use it mostly so we can play music without disturbing each other. It's as good as the pro models. Better even. We are as secure as we can get, sir."

"Ok," said Liza, as she sat on one of the mesh chairs that groaned under her weight. "First things first. I'm not the Paragon. I'm not John West. I'm Elisabeth Dunkirk."

"Uh huh," Control nodded, as he sat down.

"Uh huh? That's it?"

"Yes, sir. I mean, ma'am."

"Everyone else freaks out, and you just go, 'Uh Huh?'"

"You're not the first Paragon, ma'am. They've changed before. I've been suspicious for awhile. You've been unusually disoriented and unusually nice to me. Very out of character. I've been documenting my suspicions and reporting them to Agent One."

"Oh, great. I thought you knew Agent One was John."

"Protocol, ma'am. I'm supposed to report any issues I have about the team to Agent One. Officially, I'm not supposed to know Agent One is you, I mean John. So there was no reason not to report you to you, I mean John. Also, there are procedures in place in case the Paragon changes, and I'd come under a lot of scrutiny if that occurred under my watch, so to date I've documented everything."

"Even better," griped Liza under her breath.

"But Agent One ordered me to watch Paragon, specifically, as of this morning, and to report to him any unusual behavior."

"You just told on me, didn't you? Before we came in here."

"Yes, ma'am. I let Agent One know about the building damage and this meeting. Although I did follow your orders, and what is discussed in here currently remains private. I also feared a possible hostile action so I activated a failsafe protocol that will be engaged if I don't get back to my desk in ten minutes."

"Damn it."

"Ma'am," Control said. He was sweating and his toes were tapping on the floor. "I also request that you not harm me, as the action will be considered an act of aggression against the United States of America and NATO. As of this moment, aside from a temporary AWOL situation that is being processed through channels, you've performed the official duties of the alpha hero within the expected parameters and committed no additional crimes."

"Additional crimes? I haven't committed any crime."

"Impersonating an officer, destruction of NATO property, illegal access to federal protected materials, trespassing, and others."

"Oh, give me a break. I didn't choose any of this, and I'll pay for the damn wall. Eventually."

"You didn't report the transfer of power immediately. That alone is a federal offense."

"Seriously? John is such an ass. He told me not to. All that ass does is lie. He's also why I want to talk to you. I want to find him."

"That is not possible. The Paragon transfer is fatal to the party transferring out of the Paragon vessel."

"What?"

"If the transfer occurred, you could not have talked to him post transfer or seek him out now, because he is dead."

"So let me get this straight. You think John is dead. But you've been reporting to him, and getting orders from him, as Agent One."

"Actually I assumed someone else had assumed the mantle of Agent One. I don't speak to him directly. We communicate on an encrypted channel with voice modulation."

"Ok. Fine. John is alive. And he is in *my* body. Liza's body. The girl who was here that I asked you to track."

"But how did that…Oh! Dr. Psi! We've suspected that he has the ability to transfer hosts. We assume that is how he has avoided detection and incarceration all these years, but there is no record of him being able to transfer other persons."

"Well now there is," said Liza, as she folded her arms.

Control got up from his chair and began to pace. "That has some truly terrifying security implications." Control was silent for a time. Liza stared at him and tried to will him to talk while her teeth ground audibly. "If I assume the possibility that what you are speaking is the truth, ma'am, it does not change the fact that you impersonated the Paragon illegally. Paragon Three does not have the authority to sanction such a thing, so regardless of what he advised you to do, you have broken the law. The circumstances may work to your favor in a hearing, but I'm not a lawyer."

Liza slammed her hands on the table, cleanly breaking off a third of it. "Listen to me, you moron. John is ripping apart my life, and I want it back! The only way to do that is to find him and Dr. Psi and put it right. But John skipped out on me, and I need you to find him. Then we can find that other whack job and sort this all out."

"Except I don't work for you, and you're asking me to commit treason."

"What if Agent One is breaking the law? Huh? He stole my identity! He... I can't even say it, but he violated my friend, and I want justice! Who does he answer to? Anyone?"

"Technically, the United Nations Security Council. And under certain circumstances and actions the President of the United States or NATO command."

"Fine. We'll get them on the phone and tell them to haul his ass in here. I bet they would love to find out why they were deceived and that *he's* the one who's AWOL."

"You can't do that. There would be chaos. Paragon acts as a deterrent against several third world armies and powered soldiers in the first and second world order. If they knew you were a fake, they'd strike."

"Well, there you go. That sounds like a real crime. John stuck me with that kind of responsibility and then ran away, but he's still pulling the strings like the paranoid, power-mad, all-powerful OZ freak that he is."

A heavy silence settled between them as Liza stared Control down. "You did come to me," he said.

"Damn right I did."

"Agent One has been difficult to reach and slow to respond, and it has caused a lot of procedural problems."

"He's been doing that all along. He has his whole team blackmailed into working for him. Blurr deals with immigrant smuggling. CyberSoldier is in the closet. Cinaed, well Cinaed doesn't have a lot of choice in men given her deadly powers. He's probably got something on Shokkusan, too, just not sure what it is. But it's not just the team, it's entire countries and governments that owe him! He owns billions and doesn't give a dime to charity. He put a damn chip in *your* head. Heck, for all I know he directly controls you."

"No, he doesn't," Control answered icily.

"This is not a nice guy. Help me bring him back. You want to keep him in the suit, fine. That's your business. Just get me out of this."

"This would have to be an Agency mission. We can't have you in the field now that I know you're untrained and not cleared. I think I can arrange for house arrest until it's sorted out. Nothing too severe."

"If you don't help me, I'm going out of this room and smashing every damn computer I can find. Then I'm going to fly out of here and go look for him myself. Or do you actually have a way to stop me? Do you?"

"Threatening me isn't going to help your cause."

"I was the one who was nice to you. I came to you. *You're* the one not helping *my* cause. If you don't help me, I have to assume you're helping him. That makes you my enemy. You don't want me for an enemy."

Control swallowed and said, "You're bluffing."

"There's thirty thousand dollars of not bluffing damage upstairs. Want to go see it? Head first?"

"You wouldn't hurt me. Nothing in the psych profile I've been preparing on you indicates you would harm someone intentionally."

"Machines aren't people, computer head."

Control's eyes narrowed. "You only have a few minutes before the emergency protocols kick in and you become a fugitive."

"Damn it, Control. I came to you because you're the only one I've met who has any common sense. These heroes live in glass houses. You lead them around like trained puppies and clean up after they have accidents. Well, this is the biggest accident yet. Your man went rogue. In a *big* way. I want to help you fix it, and then I am out of your life." Liza sat back in her chair looking defeated. "I didn't ask for any of this. I just want to go home. Please?"

"I can't do that."

"Wait a minute. Why did he break into his own apartment?"

"I don't know. Presumably to get what was in his safe."

"Then why tear the rest of the place apart? He knew where to look. He could have opened the safe, closed it, left, and no one would know he was there, right?"

"Perhaps he wanted to make it look like a robbery."

"But the only person on the security records is me. If I didn't do it, it's a dead give away he did it. So that ruins any logic for making it look like a robbery, so it had to be a real robbery."

"You're suggesting someone else got in using his codes?"

"Yeah, and they wanted whatever was in those safes. And knowing the obsessive data John collects, I'll bet it was info about every Paragon before him. Why would somebody want that?"

"Well, there are missing records on Paragon One and Two, as well as sealed files."

"Do you have any idea what was in them? I think you do. I can read it on your face."

"You're not cleared to know what I know."

"So tell me what you can."

He drummed his fingers on the table, then said, "Paragon One was routinely physically examined by the military. They wanted to understand his biology so they could make their own synthetic soldiers, much the way the Nazis did. All those records were lost. He was also exposed to every toxic gas and biological weapon that was used in the Second World War. Some had some serious effects on him, though he always eventually recovered, but those test results are gone, too."

"And Paragon Two? What dirt did you have on him?"

"He was somehow forced to change into Paragon Three after a secret military tribunal found him guilty of dereliction of duty and treason. The methods and the court rulings and transcripts are missing."

"They murdered him."

"Execution. The punishment for those crimes does carry a death penalty."

"Is that what I have to look forward to when you bastards figure out I'm not a good little soldier?"

Control looked like he'd been punched in the gut. "That is a possible outcome."

"So you're signing my death warrant."

"I'm doing my job."

"Well, if I'm going down, answer me this. Who would want to know all that stuff about the Paragon? Not John. He already knew this stuff."

"Another party who wants the Paragon's power, I presume. If I accept your logic."

"Let's stick with the easy suspect. Dr. Psi. He's pissed, and I screwed up his plans. He wanted the Paragon body."

"He wouldn't have been able to get into the building."

"Unless he knew what John knows. What if he kidnapped John? What if those Agent One directives aren't coming from John, but from Dr. Psi?"

"That doesn't sound right."

"But possible, right?"

"Maybe," Control muttered.

Liza ticked off points by folding down fingers on her hand. "Someone robbed John's apartment. Someone dumped millions into my bank account. John was hiding out at my apartment and then suddenly left. John told me he doesn't want to be Paragon anymore, so he tells me to fake it while he directs things unseen as Agent One, then suddenly he stops advising me."

Control shook his head. "I don't see a point."

"Neither do I. It doesn't add up. That's the point. John is up to something, or someone is after him and up something, or both. Don't you want to know what's going on? Don't you want to know why John didn't tell you what happened?"

"Of course I want to know. Information is what I do."

"But Control is who you are, and you've got no control over any of this."

Control rubbed the bridge of his nose. "You're giving me a headache."

"Help me find him. I want my body back. I want my life back."

"If anyone is going to apprehend him, it should be the Agency."

"No deal. He has dirt on everyone, and he hired all of you. No foxes in the hen house. On the other hand, you know you can trust me. My motivation is clear." Liza held out her hands in a pleading gesture, "He's either on the run, or he's captured by Dr. Psi. Neither thing is good."

Control stared at the wall and then lightly thumped his forehead against it. "John has a safe house in Nebraska. It's off the grid in the middle of nowhere. He goes there when he's on vacation sometimes. All I know is a general locale within a hundred mile radius. It's shielded, too. Doesn't show up on satellite."

"Sounds like a good place to look. How will I find it? Can I see it? Is it underground?"

"No idea. But I've recorded enough of his approaches to get a decent vector."

Liza clapped her hands together, a bit too loudly because of her strength. "Thank you!" Control turned around and Liza could see the weight on his shoulders from his defeated posture. "How much trouble are you going to get in for doing this?"

"Depends on how this works out. I have a lot of plausible deniability. No proof you aren't John. No proof John is Agent One. I'm following orders, and you do have a standing order to find Ms. Dunkirk."

Liza got up and clapped him on the shoulders. It almost knocked him to the ground. "You have my word. I'll take all of the blame if it comes to that. You can always say I forced you, ok?"

He was silent again. "Well, you did threaten me."

"Sorry. I was desperate. I wouldn't have really smashed you into a wall. Your psych profile was right."

Control nodded. "I can do a search on contract work done in the area. Someone built it or added equipment to it. Someone hooked up electricity and supplied gas, water, and probably phones. There's a footprint somewhere."

"He has a lot of aliases."

"I've deduced all of them, I think. But in this case, an absence of information is also a clue. If I find a data hole where there shouldn't be one, then it's a smoking gun."

"How long will it take to look?" Liza asked.

"Already done," he said. "When you went AWOL, I thought you, or rather he, might be headed there. So I drew up a likely set of locations just in case Cinaed's hunch was wrong."

"Can you give me some kind of com that only you and I can talk on? If not, I'll need maps. I'm not wearing the suit again. I don't trust anyone at this point. Except you. And that's only because I have no choice."

"Wear the suit. The clothes are designed to withstand high velocity travel, even though they don't look it. I'll lock the suit out from anyone but me. But if you don't come back in twenty-four hours, I'll turn the tracker back on and send the agents after you."

"Deal. I'd look pretty stupid flying around in pajamas anyway."

"I don't really know why I'm helping you."

"Because you're a good man," Liza said hugging him as gently as she could.

"I don't think I can promise I won't change my mind."

Liza kissed him on the cheek. "You won't because you're a sweetheart."

Control recoiled in disgust and Liza let him go. Control scratched his face.

"Oh. Sorry," Liza said with an apologetic smile. "I haven't shaved. I'm a little scratchy. I'll give you a proper thank you when I have my own body back. Promise."

13

Liza, carefully avoiding hallway encounters, returned to Paragon's apartment. Once inside, she put on the cleanest uniform (verified by smell test) she could find and went to the window. Now that she thought to look, she discovered that one of the windows was set up to fly out of. It would fully open and then close on a timer, allowing her to avoid the roof. She took a glance around the room, debated about bringing Cinaed, and decided to go it alone. She took a deep breath for her nerves and flew out. She contacted Control, and he had the firewall up just before she kicked into supersonic speed.

Having Control be her guiding copilot helped immensely. Now she could fly through the clouds and high above them without having to slow and guess landmarks. She increased her speed to the most she could endure, closing her eyes and covering her ears with her hands. Control kept her on target for the most part, satellites and signals being what they were, but even the slightly inaccurate information enabled her to fly faster than she could have on her own.

Flying above the clouds, despite the pretty view, was boringly repetitive, and Liza's mind wandered. She knew now how fast Paragon was and thought about how slowly he had moved at the book signing. Questions had been tugging her in the back of her mind: How had an old, feeble man gotten past the Agency, and why was the Paragon so slow to deal with him? Also, why had Dr. Psi attacked the Paragon in public after hiding for decades? Why have an old body if he could change bodies? It wasn't adding up. Her head hurt as her thoughts went round and round. She didn't hear Control at first when he said that she was on target and it was time to slow down.

At Control's suggestion, she dropped down to fly at treetop level. This kept her below radar level, just in case John had some way of watching her approach, and it enabled her to avoid being a curious blip on civilian and military radar. The trees were scattered in clumps and property lines and that fell away entirely as she approached a large open ranch on mostly flat ground. The fields were scrubby and untended. There were no cattle or sheep, and there was no sign of farming or upkeep of any kind. Dead center in this empty expanse, accessible only by dirt roads, was an ancient farmhouse. "That building is at an eighty percent probability that it's the Paragon's safe house," said Control nervously. "He's likely to have defenses and security, so approach with caution."

"Let's just hope he's there alone and not in the clutches of Nazi grandpa," Liza said as she dropped even lower, flying just inches over the ground. It gave her an exhilarating sense of speed despite the fact that she was traveling at only a minor fraction of her previous velocity.

"Detecting interference. I may be jammed," said Control just before the com went dead.

Liza tensed as she flew right up to the porch of the two-story farmhouse and hovered in front of the door.

She paused, and nothing attacked her or otherwise happened. She took a breath, turned the antique doorknob, and found it unlocked. The hinges squealed from disuse as she opened it. Inside she could see an old wooden staircase leading up from the entrance, a parlor off to the right, and a kitchen to the left. The air was still and smelled vaguely stale and moldy, but there were no dust or cobwebs visible. The place was clean.

She drifted into the room, and the lights turned on of their own accord. They weren't ordinary lights. Every fixture was a fluorescent bulb of extremely bright white intensity, more like runway lights or stage lights than house lights. She had just turned to go back out when the lights started to strobe all at once from every direction. More lights turned on. Light fixtures were hidden in every corner and under hang, so that no place was in shadow. The interior of the building became brighter than daylight, and all of it was flashing in a synchronized strobe.

The affect on Liza was instantaneous. She fell to the ground with a loud thump, and her body thrashed and convulsed in the throes of a complex seizure. After a few moments of this, she lost consciousness altogether.

Liza awoke face up on a table, her feet touching the ground because it was angled so heavily. Her wrists were restrained by straps, as was her waist and neck. The table was made of metal and ice cold. She had no idea how she had gotten there. Her last clear memory was of flying. "Was I shot down?" she muttered. "Did I crash?" Her head was dizzy and foggy and she couldn't focus her eyes. "Control?" she asked out loud.

"Oh, do shut up, child. Ve are busy." The voice came from her right. As she turned her head, the room spun faster than she turned. The vertigo was horrible. She closed her eyes and stopped moving, but the sensation of whirling continued. She tried to hold her head, but the straps kept her arms down.

"Fuck that," she thought, as she tried to break the straps. They didn't budge. One of them pinched her skin and caused a sharp, but sobering, pain. She opened one eye to look down, and it was like looking through a dirty lens, but she could make out her hand. It looked too small and far away, the fingers tiny. She closed her eyes.

"It worked!" a voice said. It sounded like her voice. She hadn't spoken, so how was she hearing herself talk?

"Ov course it vorked! I am not an imbecile."

The second voice was wrong somehow. It wasn't old or feeble. It was strong, low-pitched, decisive, and not old and infirm. That wasn't Dr. Psi's voice; she knew that, but it sounded like him. More than just the accent, it was the bitter condescending tone. Pure bile in every word. She needed to know what was going on.

"Didn't think I would miss this, but I do. God it feels good."

"Ja, ja. Jou are vondervul. Now sit. Ve must vinish zis."
"Fine."

There were noises and shuffling and sounds she couldn't figure out. She tried to look, but a blinding bright light was now shining in her eyes. She shut her eyes quickly, but it didn't help, instead it caused a bright trail of stars to slide around her eyelids. The motion sickness returned. The gathering nausea rose up from her toes and washed over her body like a breaking wave. She dry heaved, and bitter, acidic bile got into her mouth. She tried to spit it out but only succeeded in drooling.

"Shouldn't there be an adjustment period? A break? I'm still a little weary from the first transfer. That won't affect the process?"

"Sie mind, it adapts. Now bite down on zis."

"I didn't need a mouthpiece before, why do I need one now? What are you up to?"

"Jou vere dizzy. Unt I do not vant jou to be bitink sie tongue. I am beink careful, or iz zat not gut enough vor you, Herr Colonel?"

"Colonel," thought Liza. He's talking to me. He's hearing my voice and talking to me. But I'm not talking to him, someone else is. It's someone else. Who? I should know this!

"Zere. Iz gut. Now, I must shtrap jou in. Moofment iz dangerous, ja?"

Belts clicked, and the fog in Liza's brain eased a bit. Something was itching her face, and she couldn't touch it, so she puffed at it. The second try she got the offending hair off her face and out of her mouth.

"Hair?" she thought, "in my mouth? My hair's not even an inch long!" She focused her thoughts on any sensations her body was telling her. She was hungry, thirsty, and badly craving chocolate. She hadn't had hunger pangs like this in a long, long time. She also had to pee and found it tough to hold in. She concentrated, but everything felt wrong. She flexed her arms again to break the restraints and felt her nails dig into the palms of her clenched fists. When had she last cut her nails? Not in weeks. John showed her the laser thing he used, but she couldn't figure out how to use it. She'd tried biting them once and had hurt her teeth. "Teeth," she thought and ran her tongue over them. They were uneven on one side; a canine was turned a bit and was pointier than it should have been. Braces had fixed it some, enough that they didn't call her snaggletooth anymore, but not enough to perfect it. Nothing that cheap ass dentist had ever done was right, but he was all Medicaid would cover.

"Wait. My teeth should be perfect," she thought. "Paragon's teeth are perfect!"

"Zere. All iz in place. Vee vill begin, ja?"

An sound arose, a growl of consent, but it was muffled. The voice was probably blocked by the mouthpiece that had been mentioned. It still sounded like her voice.

"*No,*" she thought, her heart suddenly pounding. "*It sounded like Paragon's voice! I'd gotten so used to it, that I thought it was me! If I'm not Paragon…*"

"You switched us back!" yelled Liza in her own voice. She knew it for sure then. She was Liza in Liza's body.

"*Shut up,*" yelled the Germanic voice from across the room.

Liza tried to open her eyes, slowly this time, and she gradually made out that she was in a living room, but the furniture was pushed to the corners and covered in cloth. In the middle of the room were machines she couldn't identify, lots of chrome and self-important blinking lights. Standing behind a large gun-like device that swiveled and pivoted on a support tripod was a very tall and very blond man. He was handsomely built and in his late teens or early twenties. His jaw was strong, he had a perfect aquiline nose, and he topped off his perfection with piercing blue eyes, assuming Nordic gods were your definition of perfection. Dr. Psi had jumped bodies into an Adonis.

The gun thing was pointing at another inclined operating table. Strapped to the table was the Paragon. His hands held some kind of device that had chords running to a machine that pulsed with the squiggle of a heart beat. Liza looked at herself, being careful to move slowly. She was wearing a pair of designer jeans and a t-shirt that was too tight on her. She also had on boots that she'd never seen before. She'd never go out looking like this.

Her mind raced to think about what had happened, but she couldn't recall anything past the point when she was flying. Control had said something about jamming. She remembered a porch. Her mind raced harder, making her dizzy, but she recalled lights flashing. "Flashing lights," she said out loud. "What did you do to me?"

The Nordic model threw up his hands, which had been calibrating some kind of dial on the gun. "Unt sie Paragon body? It iz susceptible to sie seizures under certain circumstances, ja? Now shut up. Vhy did I not bringen sie second gag? I am gettink senile again." Without even looking at her, he drew a gun from a belt holster and pointed it at her.

Liza didn't shut up. "How did you know that? Was it in the *records you stole from the safe* in Paragon's apartment?"

Paragon made a noise that sounded a little like, "What safe?"

"Nein. Das Colonel here, he knows lots ov tricks." He laughed a cold, dirty laugh that made her skin crawl. "Das I varn jou vonce more. Silence or vee vill kill jou sooner zen planned and vith more pain."

"Kill me?" Liza felt her heart pound even faster.

"Ja. Sie Colonel unt I can not be havink any loose ends about." He grinned. "So sorry…"

Liza's mind raced. "You changed bodies again. You're Dr. Psi. And you switched us back."

The man raised an old gun with a long barrel and aimed it at her. "Now I am thinkink? Quick vill be better."

Liza thought to herself, "How long have I been out? How long before Control sends in troops? This place smells like the farmhouse. If so, every second I can waste is a chance for the cavalry to arrive." Then she said out loud, "Don't shoot yet. I just want to know if I'm right."

"Vhy vould I care iv jou are right?" said the man she was certain was the new Dr. Psi.

"Because maybe I told my suspicions to others. If you kill me, you won't know what I told them."

Dr. Psi pulled back the hammer with a loud click. "So vhat."

"So, so, *so*! I told someone you and Paragon were secretly working together! That John wanted out but couldn't quit without dying in the process. But he knew that you changed bodies. So he hired you to switch him. And you did it in public to make it look like…" She floundered, but her gut was telling her she was on the right path. She had no idea why they did the switch in public though because Paragon would have ended up in the old man's body, and Dr. Psi would be Paragon, and that seemed dumb. What did John gain from that?

"Oh wait! I've got it!" she thought.

Liza said out loud, "You did it in public so Dr. Psi would be seen getting arrested. You'd never reveal what the weapon did. It would look like a power ray that failed to hurt Paragon. No one would know you switched…but…John wouldn't want to be a dying old man, so there would be a second switch, probably into the body you have now. The person in that young body would then be the one stuck in jail. You get to be the Paragon, and no one would know you're Dr. Psi, while John get's a new body. John's free of being Paragon, and he's still Agent One. You both help each other, so neither gets caught. You both win."

Dr. Psi wagged the gun around, "Unt to voo haf jou told zis fiction?"

Liza ignored him. "Bet John doesn't know you broke into his house and *stole his secret records* on the Paragon, does he?"

There was a loud bang, and Liza felt fire rip through her chest. She'd been shot. The horrible man had shot her. Her vision went white as her limbs went numb. She was going to die. For what? For wanting her life back? It was so unfair.

Paragon spit out the mouthpiece. "What were you doing in my safe? We had a deal. You do what I tell you."

"Unt leaf jou vith all sie cards? I think not!" Dr. Psi flipped a switch and a gas jet pumped dark, yellow-brown mist into the Paragon's face. His pupils collapsed to pin pricks and his eyes swelled as his body shook and rattled the restraints. Blisters appeared on his skin where the gas touched. "Did jou know sie evect mustard gas has on sie Paragon? I do," he said as he put on a gas mask that covered his own head. "Jour amazink body tries to heal sie chemical burns as zey form. But it takes all its sie resources." Paragon stopped jerking and fell limp and the blisters stopped forming. Dr. Psi turned off the gas. "As jour immune system fights, jou are veaker to a second chemical attack." He turned a dial and there was a slight hissing sound. "Unt iv zat second agent vas sodium ziopental, jou vould not resist it like normal, but instead fall into a fery persuasiff state." Paragon's body relaxed and his eyes lost focus. "Persuasiff enuv to confince jou to pass sie Paragon onto someone else. Ha! Poor number two did not stand sie chance, did he? Unt now neizer do Jou!"

"Chance," murmured Paragon, "one chance left."

"Jou vill make me sie Paragon. Jou vill tell me all ov jour secrets, unt I vill haf *all* sie cards. I *vin*." Dr. Psi turned his attention to Liza. "It vill take a moment vor sie drug to vork, so I vill talk to jou, mine dear fraulein." He walked over and slapped her face. "Jou are dyink, ja? Sie bullet has struck jour kidney. Iz painvul. Toxic body vaste iz killing jou. Tell me voo jou talked to, unt I vill safe jou."

Liza couldn't focus past the pain and the dizziness. She heard all that was said, but it was like they were a million miles away. She couldn't talk if she wanted to.

Dr. Psi slapped her again, but got no response. "Oh vell. Next." He walked over to Paragon just as a third mist canister evacuated and filled the air. "Unt zat neutralizes sie Mustard Gas. My own infention. Vas wery usevul in sie Var." Dr. Psi removed his mask. His voice took on a patronizing and syrupy tone like a fiend offering candy to a child. "Now, mine gut vriend. Jou vish to help me, ja? Zen you *vill* make me sie Paragon."

Paragon said in a coughing, throat-burnt voice, "You double crossed me."

"Nein. Jou vanted me to do zis. Jou vanted *me* to be sie Paragon. Jour puppet, ja! Vhat jou did not know iz zat I cannot risk svitchink bodies any more. Each svitch degrades sie host. Like sie DNA replication, each copy iz imperfect. Errors are introduced. Zis causes hormone changes zhat induce rapid aging, cancers, unt senility! I had vone gut change levt unt I vasted it on Hans. Hans vas for *jou!*" Dr. Psi stroked Paragon's cheek, lovingly. "But jou are my gut vriend. So jou must help me now, in my time of need, ja?"

"You'll kill me," Paragon said in a slurred voice.

"Nein. I von't be sie vone. It vill be jou. Jou vill pay for all jou haf done. Jou vill hurt jou, but jou vill help me. Jour sins vill be gone unt jou vill help me. Iz such a gut plan, ja?"

Dimly, the head of the Paragon nodded and lolled loose on his neck.

"Gut boy. Reach vithin. Make it right. Make all zings right. Release jourselv vrom sie burden of sie Paragon. Release it. Keep jour vord. Make it right."

A blueish white aura of energy began to ooze out of John's skin and mist about him like a cloud.

"*Ja!* Zis iz gut. More! Release it! Be vree!"

"Free," murmured John as his chest made a light rattling sound and his body fell limp.

"Vhat is zis?" Dr. Psi flexed his arms and made big gestures. "I do not veel diverent!"

Snapping sounds came from behind him, and a groan. Dr. Psi turned and saw Liza clutching her wound with one hand, and with the other, holding the table in the air like it weighed nothing.

"You have the right to remain silent," Liza said, swinging the table like a tennis racket, smacking Dr. Psi like a tennis ball, sending him across the room to bounce off the wall, leaving a dent in the plaster. "Because I am sick of listening to your shit."

She tossed the table aside and walked haltingly over to where the Dr. had hit the ground. She grimaced with each step from the bullet wound, but the pain was fading rapidly.

Dr. Psi gingerly pulled a remote out of a pocket and pushed the button. The lights in the room blossomed into bright white and began to strobe.

Liza closed her eyes. "Not this time."

Liza lifted him up by his neck and held him in the air as he struggled. One hand tried in vain to break her grip after dropping the remote, while the other hand brought the gun up to point at Liza's face. He fired at point blank range.

There was a roar, and a force snapped Liza's head back. Reflexively, Liza slammed him backwards into the wall. She let go of him and reached around for the remote, flailing about where she thought she had heard it fall. After a long, frantic moment, she found it. She clicked buttons at random until the lights stopped flashing behind her eyelids. Squinting, she looked out and saw Dr. Psi limp and embedded several inches into the plaster of the wall.

Liza went over to John, checked for a pulse, and listened to his chest, but she heard nothing. He was dead.

After another long moment, she closed his eyes for him. "Thanks for asking if I wanted this."

Liza twisted up some of the sheets covering the furniture. She wrapped one around Dr. Psi as if she were swaddling a baby and then twisted another into ropes to tie him up. She tightened the knots until he groaned.

She went back to John. His face and chest began to blister more as the chemical burns took hold. "Now what do I do? You messed up my life and yours."

"Be you. That's good enough."

Liza looked at John, but he hadn't spoken. She checked his pulse again and found none. The voice that spoke was his. She heard it.

"I'm fading. The transfer."

Liza looked around and then realized the voice was in her head. "John?"

"I can see now. What you've done." The voice was breathy and halting and it grew weaker and more distant with each word. "I know now. How you think. You're not me. You're better. Better than me... you're the hero... fate... karma's a..."

Silence. She waited.

Nothing more was said.

Flashes of memories danced before her eyes, random images from the lives of all three Paragons. No feelings, no thoughts, just images. She saw scenes of heroics and tragedies, all intertwined, a highlight reel of the highs and lows of each of their lives, but out of order and out of context. They blurred together and became hard to grasp, like a dream upon waking. Then the images, like John's voice, were gone.

She hated him, hated him so much but she cried. Huge torrents of tears, some of frustration, some of genuine sympathy for his passing.

When her tear ducts ran dry, she sniffed and wiped her eyes. Pondering what to do next, she looked around the room.

Trying not to be repulsed, and mostly failing, she pulled off John's shirt. It burned a little, so she took it to the bathroom and turned on the water. The pipes rattled and then brownish water came out in a dribble. She washed the shirt as best as she could. Then, with a disgusted look, she put the shirt on over the one she was wearing. It roughly fit her, though in a completely different way. She looked down at the stained white star on her chest and tapped the com system on, but it only produced static. She dimly recalled it being jammed, and with a leap, she flew into the air and poured on the juice to punch through the ceiling, through the bedroom above, and then through the roof creating a rain of scattered shingles in her wake. She flew up, until the clouds were below her and the com came back to life.

"Paragon to Control. We have a situation. Send in the boys for a cleanup at my location. I'll be waiting for you. Paragon Four, out."

She flew back down and sat on Dr. Psi until the agents arrived.

EPILOGUE

It was a week before Liza was able to go home. In the interim, she was interviewed several dozen times by generals and spooks and even by the President. It all felt surprisingly normal to her. She told the truth to everyone, and each time the other side was surprised by her candor. She let it all wash over her, and, in the end, all of them said something to the effect of, "Welcome aboard. I look forward to working with you." She'd nod and shake hands and go on to the next debriefing or interview. One thing she learned was that they had all hated John, and they were all afraid of her.

When she met the President, she resigned as Agent One, or rather declined to be him. The President had no idea what she was talking about, but he assured her he'd look into it.

The Agency handled the press, and they kept the media out of the whole affair, which, of course, fed the gossip hounds and that made the rumors wilder and more elaborate. CyberSoldier helped sidetrack the press by coming out in a very public speech, where he introduced his life partner and announced his divorce at the same time. Cinaed was with him and had some boy-toy on her arm to assure everyone she was just fine with this.

The Agency took all the chaos in stride, and Liza wondered if anything rattled them. They were all polite to her, and she was certain they were nicer to her than they had been to John. The rest of the team relaxed around her, too. Everyone had been so used to walking on eggshells and being buttoned up.

Liza refused to stay in John's apartment when they offered it to her and arranged to give it to Cyber instead. Liza then moved in with Cinaed. Cinaed's apartment actually had two separate bedrooms, so it worked out nicely. It could have used three, because Shokkusan effectively moved in, and the three gals would talk and joke and drink deep into the night.

Without a word, the Blurr quit and was not heard from again.

Liza also made it a point to visit Control in person every day. She also kept her com on and joked and chatted with him constantly when not in meetings. He always tried to call her ma'am or Colonel but she made him call her Liza. She made him blush a lot and laugh, and she made a private bet with herself how long it would take for him to realize he now had a girlfriend. She figured it would be a few months at his rate of cluelessness. For that matter, she'd never had a long-term boyfriend, so she was fine with taking it slow.

There was no formal ceremony to make her the fourth Paragon, but when UNSAD Agents 33 and 34 brought Liza her new uniform, it finally felt real. Cinaed and Shokkusan wanted to design her suit, but Liza would have nothing to do with their taste in spandex clothes. She kept the Paragon's reinforced jeans, but went with flats instead of boots. Her top was a simple blouse in pink with a white star patterned onto the front. It was too girly for her, but she'd chosen it on purpose. The uniform wasn't for her; it was for the world. It was meant to make a statement: "There's a new gender in town." She also planned to change the look from time to time. No way was she going to have a closet filled with the same thing.

Her body was different now that she was the Paragon. Her metabolism changed, and she got a bit thinner, despite eating whatever she wanted. When she went to the gym, her body toned easily. She grew taller, then taller still. Before long she hardly recognized herself in the mirror. So much for the Paragon's looking alike. Maybe there'd never been a female one before, or maybe John lied like he lied about everything.

Back home, the Agency had quietly moved a detail in that provided round-the-clock security to her family, and by Liza's insistence, to Gwen. Liza wanted them to hear the news from her first, so the security was kept covert, at least at first. That allowed her some time before going home, but she couldn't put it off forever. This time she followed all the procedures and protocols before she left, mainly to stall. This was going to be difficult.

She rehearsed what she'd say to them as she streaked across the country. Control tried to be helpful and had prepared some talking points for her, but she politely ignored him. He was brilliant at getting things done, but clueless when it came to people. She decided, right then, to make it a point to see if dating him could help fix that.

As Liza flew, she thought about her mom and what she would say to the woman who had thought so little of her all her life. Liza decided to just be nice, it was the right thing to do. She'd seen enough darkness and suffering in the world. She had no interest in adding to it. Besides, if mom was a pain, Liza knew she could always fly away.

Liza landed on Gwen's porch and her hand trembled when she put her key into the door. This was going to be a lot to talk about, and Gwen would want every detail so that she could tell the story over and over again and warp and twist it in her own way. As Liza opened the door, she decided to ask Gwen to move to New York with her. She didn't know if Gwen would go to a big city, but Two Tales didn't have much keeping her here. Then Liza thought about what John had done and was instantly and almost violently ill. It was not going to be a pleasant talk.

As she walked up the stairs to Gwen's floor, she made a solemn promise to herself to always do the right thing, no matter what, no matter how hard it was, because that was the kind of person she wanted to be. She was going to be the kind of person who would make things right, no matter what happened. She would make things right for Gwen, for the team, for everyone.

Who could stop her? She was the Paragon.

THE END

ABOUT THE AUTHOR

I was born in the summer of love in 1967, and I've been a writer since I first learned how to string words together - but I haven't been an author. An author finishes works they've started. Instead of becoming an author, I had a career and a family and along the way I accumulated a drawer full of incomplete works.

My first novel was an accident. Variants of this story had been floating around in my head for years as novels "to-be" that never became. The various story bits and subplots found their way into my comic book scripts but the core story remained unused. I thought I was done with this material, that it had no place in a finished work. Then, after writing some two dozen comic scripts, I was itching to get back into prose so I cracked my knuckles and sat down to write whatever came to mind. What came out of that exercise was the first draft of this very book.

The moral to this story is that life is a journey - as long as you keep on walking, you'll end up somewhere you wanted to be.

ABOUT THE COVER PHOTOGRAPHER

In the autumn of the leap year of 1968, just 15 days after NASA launched Apollo 7, Anthony Redell entered our world. He brought to our gray existence a whimsical sense of humor and he shares with all of us his enduring love of science fiction and photography.

In his own modest words, "There was very little of interest in the world prior to that fateful date of October 26th 1968. And a fateful day it was! Based on the gnostic mastery of numerological magic, one can deduce that October 26th was the 299th day of that calendar year and observe that it is an odd number. However, had this been a normal year, and not a cosmological leap year, this would have been the 300th day, which is an even number. The strangeness continues, for October is the 10th month of the year, but the origin of the term October in Latin means eight. What evil lurks in the heart of men to invent such artifice to conspire to obscure a date utilizing such occult occlusions?" Given this, it is perhaps needless to point out that Anthony was born a true Scorpio, or that his very name was obscured in childhood as Nitney. He laughs maniacally at all of this, "If you were born and raised like I was, it is nigh impossible to be normal. You are either destined for greatness; or at the least a peculiar kind of oddness."

In 2006, Anthony created Heavenly Light Productions, LLC where he specializes in photography. When he works with artists and models, it is for the pure fun and pleasure to be found in creating epic images, and in the joy of meeting wonderful people.
"It is a true honor and privilege for me to work with such a talented author and professional. Scott Bachmann shares a driving love for words and his fanboy dream of comics as I do for photography." – Anthony Redell